Books by Peter De Vries

No But I Saw the Movie
The Tunnel of Love
Comfort Me With Apples
The Mackerel Plaza
The Tents of Wickedness
Through the Fields of Clover
The Blood of the Lamb
Reuben, Reuben
Let Me Count the Ways
The Vale of Laughter
The Cat's Pajamas & Witch's Milk
Mrs. Wallop
Into Your Tent I'll Creep

Into Your Tent I'll Creep

Into Your Tent I'll Creep

Peter De Vries

Little, Brown and Company
Boston – Toronto

LIBRARY OF CONGRESS CATALOG CARD NO. 70–161422

FIRST EDITION

T10/71

Published simultaneously in Canada
by Little, Brown & Company (Canada) Limited

PRINTED IN THE UNITED STATES OF AMERICA

Into Your Tent I'll Creep

1

It wasn't until I had become engaged to Miss Piano that I began avoiding her. On the street, in supermarkets, almost everywhere you could imagine. I even gave her a wide berth at parties. Someone has said that "No date has been set for the wedding," is the finest sentence in the English language. My feet on the occasions I'm naming did my thinking for me. There was no conscious decision. Ducking into doorways and scuttling around corners at her approach seemed a forthright and natural thing to do, as simple and natural as slipping a ring on a woman's finger.

One afternoon in particular I'm sloping along up

Stony Island Avenue, one of our more arterial South Side Chicago streets, when I spot her bearing down on me with her brisk stride, swinging the briefcase bulging with translations of Racine and looking more like Burt Lancaster than I had really bargained for, and bang! I dodge into the nearest doorway. Ah, sweet mystery of life, at last I find you. Here is a guy bolting from his oncoming betrothed like a criminal on the lam, his legs taking him over a puddle and onto the cement stoop of a dingy entrance hall in one long leap. An instinct obeyed in a flash, over in a flash — one with the involuntary start, the unplanned guffaw.

Here, flattened against a row of apartment-house doorbells, like the breasts of girls just beginning to be nubile don't you know, in a musty passage cluttered with prams and smelling of fried steaks, I can review my present mode of life. I sit in the dark at my place pretending I'm not home. I let the phone ring on and on. I leave letters unanswered. All this is not in my best vein. Worse is yet to come. I avert my eyes from the route numbers of busses I board at random, the better not to know where they might be taking me, and so wind up in strange taverns in remote parts of the city.

"What you're doing is dismantling your identity," a guy in one of these watering troughs I had confided something of my behavior to told me. I had trouble following this line of explanation, being a bit tempest-tossed for more reasons than one. I had just had a nasty intestinal bug, and my insides still felt like a blown-out inner tube. "You're pulling the old Tinker Toy apart and

4

putting the spindles and spools together in fresh molecular combinations is all. Come, let's go outside. There seems to be a drama."

On the sidewalk the lesser of two cartoon combatants was hugging the other in a dance that would take them slowly toward the curb. "When," he puffed. "All I ast you was *when* shall the night be filled with music, and the cares that infest the Arabs and one thing and another. Everybody knows that last verse, right? But what goes before, *that you need to know to understand it*? Not one person in a thousand can tell you."

"Then why pick on me for not knowing — and my missus? Just because she's a schoolteacher and ought to, was what you were insinuating. She teaches Home Ec, you meathead!"

"Wait! Hold it. Easy now. I di'n't mean any offense. We'll put it up to these gentlemen." The question was posed to our circle of watchers, two of whom were holding the fighters' coats. "Any of you guys know the context of this very famous poem? Just *why* the night shall be filled with music, finally? The point of the whole thing?"

We all shook our heads, including my analyzer, a pale towhead who rolled his eyes and said he hoped he was too educated ever to have read Longfellow.

"There, you see?"

"That's what I'm *saying*, for Christ's sakes," said the guy who took offense. "Nobody knows. So why cast aspersions on me and my missus. Why, I ought to —"

"That's what I *mean*. So I couldn't possibly be casting

5

aspersions for that reason," said the other from the gutter, to which he had retreated after disentangling himself from the embrace. "Wait! Hold it. I di'n't know about the context myself till late this afternoon, I swear. I swear it by Almighty God. My kid came home from school and told me. Well, it's a funny thing," he said, addressing us all again. "See, the poet is knocking the bards sublime, oh not knocking them exactly, that at the end of the day when you've had it, it's not them you want, the grand old masters. No, what you want is 'some simple heartfelt lay.' See?"

"I know it's what I want," pipes up some moron with a laugh. "Nothing like cutting yourself a nice little slice of poontang when day is done."

"*Then* the night shall be filled with music, and so forth and so on. See? That O.K.? Hah? We all squared away?"

"I ought to belt you one," said the guy whose wife taught Home Ec, backing into his outheld coat. We broke it up and traipsed back inside. "Wisenheimer," he continued muttering as he rejoined his wife, whose worried head protruded from the edge of a booth like a cuckoo stuck in a clock. "People try to have a good time, few drinks in peace, and some ignorant sonofabitch always has to . . ."

This was all part of the background whose immediate memories emotionally charged the moment when I hid in the hallway listening to Miss Piano's footsteps slowing, slowing as they drew near. Or at least so I imagined. My God! had she seen me? I hastily throw together a plan. If she does stop, turn, and ask, in that pedagogical tone she can take, "Well, Albert Ernest Banghart, just exactly what is the meaning of this, may I ask?", if that happens I know what I'll do. I'll just pop from cover and say, "Boo." I was only playing, only having some hacks with her whom I have gone forth to seek in the streets of the city, saying unto the watchmen thereof, "Saw ye her whom my soul loveth, even my beloved who is unto me as a bundle of myrrh, whose eyes are as the pools of Heshbon I believe it is and whose nose is like the tower of Lebanon which looketh toward Damascus?"

Something worse happens. She hasn't seen me at all. She strides right on by, swinging the briefcase, *and I let her*.

A variation of this occurred a week later in the same general neighborhood, where we both lived, so our running into each other would in itself be no coincidence. I'm walking home from the drugstore with a bag of purchases and again I spot her coming toward me with her confident stride, swinging the Racine-jammed briefcase against her flapping flannel skirt and spanking the pavement with her "sensible" shoes. Without a moment's hesitation I take off across the street to the other side. Through dense traffic I weave, and, the sounds of demolition splitting the air, hightail it straight on toward a bus which happens to be making a stop at the corner just then, and which starts forward with a lurch that sends me sprawling up the aisle. My behavior I justify by remembering how she spells it 'bus — short for

7

omnibus — as she writes 'phone because it's short for telephone. Can you be happy with a woman who does that, to say nothing of love letters infested with semi-colons? *She can talk semicolons.* You know they're there, in those well-constructed sentences. But grabbing the bus in itself was to make it all look valid. I mean that will be the "rational explanation" *this* time in case the bride-elect has piped her swain and is now standing there with her mouth open like a flabbergasted figure in a frame of a comic strip saying "What the —?" I have to laugh at the picture (your unplanned guffaw) even as I pick myself up out of the aisle and dust myself off, to the amusement of others.

I sink into the last remaining seat in the bus with no idea where it's taking me at this insane speed, only breathing heavily as I think: "Is this man matrimonial timber?" Because what I'm doing is not good courtship. It's hardly accepted romantic custom. Yes, I was beginning to get bad vibes now from all this behavior, which no longer seemed "natural," and which was repeated at close enough intervals to be fairly considered a pattern.

A counter-impulse now seizes me. I get off at the next stop and make for a public phone booth.

"I've got to see you," I tell her in a hollow voice.

"*Now?*"

"Now."

"I only just came in the door. I haven't even got my coat off."

"Take it off."

"I've got to go out again in a minute. In fact I've already started a tub."

"Before you took your coat off?"

"Yes. I *am* in rather a rush. Hear?" She holds the phone out in order to transmit the sound of drumming water, as though her lover is some suspicious character who must be perpetually reassured he's not caught up in a web of intrigue and deception. An absolute and utter huggermugger. "Look, can't it wait until tomorrow? We have a date then, you know. The Pendletons' party; don't forget it. You did get on with Florence the other night, didn't you?"

"That the woman who went on about Villa-Lobos?"

"Not the way it's pronounced, you. It's Veeyah Lohboz."

"It's the way she pronounced it, so I naturally thought she was talking about some country place of theirs."

"Oh, Al. Or wait. He's Brazilian, where they speak Portuguese rather than Spanish. So it could be Veelah," said my linguist.

"Anyway they do have one somewhere, I think Lake Geneva, because she was telling us how they run up there for a weekend to get some rest and find these seemingly ghastly kids of theirs and their friends sacking out, and not in school at all. The boy goes to Exeter where he's learning to laugh drily."

"Tuckie. He and Eleanor have both dropped out."

"I gather the Pendletons don't mind that. It's their dropping in they can't take. The way I get it, the children will all be home for the Holidays but they're determined not to let it spoil their Christmas."

Miss Piano giggled. "I love you; but my tub runneth over."

"This is urgent. I'm right down here on Stony Island." I held the phone out the door of the booth so she could hear the rumble of traffic.

"Oh, all right. If you can come right on up. And don't stay too long."

"Don't worry."

Walking the short distance to her pad, I reviewed the party which was a pool of blood for other reasons than that you thought Villa-Lobos was somebody's country estate. And this a bash where your fiancée was showing off her catch. Hearing some cat from New York speaking about the local port authority I naturally thought he was talking about another wine expert. Christ, they had all been going at it twenty to the dozen about recent vintages, quantity discounts at the French source, what "travelled well" and what not. My mixup was perfectly understandable, especially with this kind of surrealist connection in my mind with these case lots all sloshing around in the holds of these incoming ships they were going on about, as members of those international buying clubs that are all the rage. By the time it got through to me that they were referring to officials gumming up these arrivals with harbor regulations I had already remarked, "I had a grandfather who was an expert on Madeira. At least so he thought." This drew a yack out of all proportion, my intended pretending with a brave little smile that the humor had been conscious. "Darling, where did you ever *find* him?" How would you like to be priceless, through no fault of your own? By the end of the evening the tight little smile looked like something being held together with a rubber band.

For this I had gone to the trouble of making a careful toilet, not wearing brown shoes with a blue suit or blue pants with a brown coat, pasting down an unruly cowlick and brushing not only my teeth but my tongue, as doctors now recommend for personal hygiene and social closeups. When I woke up the next morning with the hangover you can imagine, the nap on it looked like a problem in lichen identification. I still brush my tongue till I gag, twice a day, rain or shine. It's a good habit to get into, provided you don't let the organ in question, a pretty odd number, become an obsession, as it did with me when I first discovered it, there in my mouth. For weeks I was conscious of it flipping around in other people's when they talked, no aid to paying serious attention to what they're saying. One entire Shakespearean production was reduced to absurdity by the thought of all that exalted verse hinging on this pink tab flipping away in everyone's head onstage. Of course the obsession eventually wore off, but at the party in question I was still thinking in terms of guests' tongues as a component in the laughter I seemed to be inspiring through no fault of my own. Especially in the case of a guy named Merton, a bluestocking, whom I wanted to invite to step outside. Then we would see who was a primitive. I would be glad to take that buster apart. I would leave him pretty evenly distributed. And damn well put a stop to his imitations of Claude Rains. "Meet me in hahf an ah. I want to toak chew."

The door of her apartment was open when I got there and she called to me from the bathroom to come in. Sitting on the edge of the tub while she bathed, I briefed her on what had been going on to date, the mysterious doings, the conduct that seemed to leave something to be desired, to me at least. She appeared more interested in her bath than the clean breast I was trying to make of things, lolling back in the suds as she lathered now one then the other outstretched arm. "If you wanted to see me as badly as you said on the telephone," she said, "then why didn't you hail me when you saw me on the street just now?"

"That's *what* I want to see you *about*. The fact that I didn't want to, under the circumstances I'm trying to describe. There have now been two such occasions, as I'm trying to make you understand. Who can say there won't be more. Or that there won't be other variations of this thing." I flapped a hand. "I can't guarantee it."

"Nobody's asking for guarantees — or giving any," she answered, with remarkable cool. *Sang-froid* I believe it's called in what is her second language. "You know I'm against all these hypocritical pledges of eternal devotion. Writing each other checks for a million dollars when most of us are lucky to have twenty-five cents in the bank. Instead of starting out with this best-foot-forward façade that leads to inevitable disillusionment, how much more charming to level with each other. Tell one another the worst so there'll be nothing but pleasant surprises. Have I ever told you my uterus is in upside-down?" and lowered her head in what threatened to be another of her famous laughing fits.

"This may be a very heathen view of marriage."

"No, it's the heathen who are uptight; we've got to limber it up. Anything but that it's made in heaven."

"I must say you don't seem very upset."

She lowered her sponge into the water and looked thoughtfully at the wall.

"I've crossed the street to avoid people I liked; I didn't want to see them just then. Or sometimes it's those we want most to make a good impression on whom we evade; like at a party, for fear of not doing so. I'll give you my Proust with a passage marked about all this. When I was a little girl in the seventh grade, I was so hopelessly in love with a boy — Billy Round was his name — that I ran away every time I saw him coming. That sick with adoration I was."

"It's not the problem here."

I walked to the parlor, still swinging my bag of drugstore purchases, and waited there while she dried herself and got into a bathrobe. When she came in, carrying some nail-polishing paraphernalia, I was gazing between her Mondriaan draperies into the street below, scene of some of the recent mysterious goings-on.

"I wonder if my behavior — popping into doorways,

bolting at the very sight of you and one thing and another — could have its roots deep in some racial unconscious business."

"Forget the racial unconscious," she said, settling herself on the sofa. "Forget I ever told you about it. Curse
the racial unconscious, may I never hear its name
again," she went on through lips drawn into a tight
"O" as she concentrated on the task of painting her
nails.

"Something about its being bad luck to see the bride
before the wedding."

"But we're not getting married for a year!"

"Oh, I think we'll up that date. But I'm not talking
about arranged dates, like tomorrow night. I mean more
like accidental encounters with the bride-to-be, which
are frowned on in certain lands," I said, really impro-
vising a folk custom as a sort of ploy. But there was one
of which I was sure, having picked it up in a conversation I didn't think she'd been in on. "Something like the
taboo against setting eyes on the mother-in-law, which
anthropologists tell us men will go miles out of their
way to avoid in some cultures. In the most mountainous
terrains."

I held myself rigid, absolutely determined that for
once I had told her something, in this case a bit of in-
formation I got from a woman with her hair skun back
into a doughnut. But my own answered, dipping her
brush into the bottle, "Yes, a primitive taboo often interpreted as a fear or hatred of the mother-in-law —
that ogre as we still think of her — when certain au-

14

thorities say it may very well be the precise opposite, a ceremonial of respect. I mean tribal courtesy for a new family branch that could be of help in time of trouble." I silently mouthed a single expletive to myself. She screwed the cap on the bottle and set it aside. "Look, would it make you feel any better if I told you that I saw you on the street too just now, and was relieved to see you scram?"

"Then we're both in this together," I said, turning back from the window. "Up to our necks."

"We have a lot in common." She glanced at the clock and rose to show me to the door, toward which I could only move in that case. "That's important in a marriage."

"But I thought it no more than fair to tell you what's been going on. This possible storm warning, that marriage may not be my bag?"

"Well, we're all ambivalent about so many basic things. It's a universal trait."

"And another word I won't have to look up. Ambivalence, that something else that's O.K. with your intellectual friends? They disparage everything and disapprove of nothing." She shot me a look of surprise, even mild alarm. But I wasn't about to tell her I had swiped the aphorism, or where. *Let* life be full of pleasant little surprises then. I smiled and patted her hand, which was resting on the open door in readiness to close it behind me. "Then you're of two minds about me too?"

"At least."

I counted it a victory of sorts to have come away

15

without the Proust. You hack, burn, slug, and taking frequent rests finally beat your way out of one sentence, only to think, "Oh, Christ, here comes another." But I was carrying down into Stony Island with me a load of doubts heavier than those left behind. Her two-for-a-quarter words reminded me all too much of my mother. The same tendency to intellectualize everything. My mother couldn't talk about menstruation, no. She had to call it lunar periodicity, thereby taking all the fun out of it. Ambivalence was good. In one sense any man could take pride in winning a woman who was such a brain. But to be embarking on a marriage that was therefore necessarily bound to be your Pygmalion theme in reverse . . .

Downstairs on Stony Island Avenue again, however, an unexpectedly pleasant encounter drove these gloomy thoughts quite out of my head. I spotted an old flame on the other side of the street and quickly galloped across to greet her. I caught her sleeve just as she turned abruptly to window-shop, oddly enough at an agency for diesel engines which you'd hardly think she was in the market for. I didn't bother to inquire about this, or give it a second thought, so ecstatic was I at running into her like this.

"Betty Cudlipp!"

"Al Banghart, as I live and breathe. So what's new with you?"

"Nothing much. How about a quick one at Feeley's?"

2

The order my fiancée tells me underlies all seeming chaos sure lurks at the heart of this street encounter. To me there was nothing *but* pattern in bumping into Betty Cudlipp just then, because the path to my threatening marriage led straight from that old flame. It was to the ex-dilly that I would owe my wife, if any, albeit thanks to a sordid tangle you'd be put to it to find anything but chaos in. In fact you'd have to be me to know there was an underlying thread. The dilly didn't know it, the bride-elect didn't know it, and I prayed to God neither would ever learn the connection between them. This is the story of a man glad to beat all the dirt he has

17

to out of his rug provided you leave undisturbed what he's swept under it.

So it's late Sunday night in Betty Cudlipp's front parlor, a few years back. The lights are low, and I'm trying to take silk, as I believe our British cousins call it. No amount of refined, now, euphemism will soften Betty toward the sort of attempt being made, though, she's sorry. The adolescent quest for gash is just that, by whatever other name you call it. All the erogenous zones are off-limits, save for the two lips. Add to this the fact that her kiss is like a brief portion of Scripture and you wonder why I bother. Because she has the most ravishing figure imaginable, and I feel it's only a matter of time. I mean till she stops prying my hand off her flank and saying, "You World Federalists are all alike." How about a breather?

Men who pride themselves on knowing women like the back of their hand have probably got the back of one of theirs at one time or other, not a bad source of instruction. Not that I mean that in any but the figurative sense. Betty had a touch as delicate as strudel crust, even when she was saying you nay. But there is one very lusty side to her. She loves to laugh, and when she does her collective glories are like a cluster of pealing bells. The ability to supply a little out-of-pocket humor is an absolute requirement in a boy friend, as it will be in a husband, what the French call a *sine qua non*. So now. By way of having a cigarette in the dark with her, I sets fire to two Camels and then, instead of passing her one like Paul Henreid to Bette Davis in that famous movie, I sits there with a dead pan puffing away at both gaspers, leaning back with my legs crossed and one arm slung along the back of the sofa, the fags hanging down off my lip like a pair of tusks and smoke issuing from every nostril. "So how's your mother's arthritis? Oh, I'm glad to hear that. And tell me, does your father still sharpen skates on the side, bring in a little extra money? That cousin of yours from Milwaukee, is she still so tall?" This Betty deal is in absolute hysterics by the time I finally hand her cigarette over to her. Scarcely able to smoke it. She takes a drag and then, suddenly sobered, says, "What's that?"

In the silence you can hear a faint rustling noise. "Sounds like a mouse," I say. It is in fact the wrapper from my cigarette pack, which I have just wadded up and dropped in an ashtray on a nearby table, where it is now slowly expanding again, the way cellophane will. I know that's what it is, but I sense what Betty fears, and that my answer will pay off. It does indeed. It reduces her to a quivering, yielding pulp in my arms — a temptress who hadn't known she was that.

One of many. For I adopted the cellophane trick as a regular technique. Many's the candy bar or cigarette wrapper I furtively dropped behind the sofa or into a nearby corner, where as it unclenched it would generally produce the rustling noise so easy to mistake for that of mice on their rounds along the floorboards or nibbling away at the lathes in the wall. "What's that?" the dilly would say, and I'd say, "Probably a mouse," and have another clinging to me in a trembling embrace.

19

The role of manly protector is an extra thrill in its own right.

Not that the ruse always worked, or that you even had a chance to use it every time. When I phoned Tut Carpenter to make a date for later in the week and was told in her breathless fashion, "Why don't you come up right now if you're not busy," I knew the evening was a gift horse. Her brother Artie was on hand, and so was a guitar-strumming rock singer who called himself The Stopped Up Sink.

The whole worst-foot-forward vogue of goon looks and senseless names for both groups and singles was at its height then and typified in this minstrel, who wore patched dungarees, shoes made out of decayed manure, and a denim shirt unbuttoned down to his navel, from which you kept your eyes averted for fear it might be as urgently in need of grooming as his nails. Unintelligibility was his third abrasive, but you were grateful for that after catching a few snatches of the lyrics he sang, which were his own composition. He was serenading the Carpenters when I arrived, and after settling myself at Tut's feet, resigned to being part of the "court" she liked to hold in improvised open-house evenings like this, center of a gay set, I was grateful for Artie.

He had been the class brain in Southeast High, a straight-A student for whose Chicago street diction not even four years of college in Ohio had done anything. An intellectual talking like a mugg is an odd thing, but there were several in my Chicago past, all born and raised on the wrong side of the tracks like me, now also out of good schools and all sounding like Artie. De trouble wit Norwegian drama. De liquefactions of Debussy. De voisatility of Picasso. No? I say yes. That was what issued not only out of Artie's mouth but out of the side of it at that, as though he's slipping you a tip on the fourth at Arlington instead of an informed fine point. And music and art weren't even his field, electronics was. Of course my diction is no better, but there's no contrast with what I'm saying. I have no brains and I don't know anything. His sister Tut — with whom I had suddenly decided to be gravelled — had attended an eastern women's college where her accent was bevelled down by a speech department using diction recordings like emery wheels on its charges, so that she came out completely neutral, and colorless by comparison wit her picturesque brudder from whose lips fell nuances in dis Gashouse Gang brogue, which can remain as thick and permanent as a Scotchman's burr. I remember what he said about The Stopped Up Sink when the troubadour finally split, leaving us free to talk about him.

"De anti-poetic in our time has a longer pedigree dan dese yahoos tink, wit deir amusing efforts to shock de bourgeoisie which is itself as old as de hills," Artie explained, while Tut nodded with knowing baby-doll blinks that made me extra content to write her off. "De anti-poetic began, let's not forget, in poetry itself. When Eliot opened *Prufrock* wit a metaphor likening de evening sky to a patient etherized upon a table, anti-style, counter-beauty was in. As for 'de new irreverence,' my God, dat's half a century old too. It was in *De Waste*

Land dat Eliot's systematic deflation of de classics anticipated de name bands shooting de Schubert to me
Hubert and jazzing up Bach and what not in de twenties. Of course in a larger sense it goes back to Baude-
laire and beyond, but I mean for us, in our time, dis
cycle of calculated coarseness, of trowing it all away,
don'tcha know, began in Eliot. 'I have measured out my
life wit coffee spoons' is a memorable line of poetry
witout a poetic woid in it. Yes, it was poetry dat troo
poetry out de winda. Eliot meets de ultimate definition
of genius: somebody who influences people who never
hoid of him."

That was midnight or later. Now The Stopped Up
Sink was still bawling away at the top of his lungs,
"using the guitar as basically a percussion instrument," his mouth a good place to throw old razor
blades:

> *Giddle gad so buzzly, baby,*
> *Lemme grock ya frinks.*
> *All a sizmagaufry maybe,*
> *You're a most gabrinks.*

I *tried* to have mixed feelings about him, but no go. I
don't remember what his real name was, if I ever heard
it. He wanted to be known by his professional one — of
which this was the fourth or fifth. He kept changing it,
experimenting with new ones, in an effort to shake the
jinx that seemed to hound his albums. He had first
called himself The Volcanic Rock, then changed it to

Roger the Lodger, Old Newspapers, and The Wines of
Italy, in hopes of changing his image and his luck, without success. His releases sold less and less, never getting
even a smell of the Top Twenty.

After serenading us into the small hours he glanced
at his wristwatch, as though it might be time to be getting back into the crypt. Then I sensed Tut smiling in
my direction.

"Al, you used to sing," she said, causing me to grind
my teeth. "Sing something for us."

A general flurry of coaxing, with some show of de-
mocracy from The Stopped Up Sink that made me
laugh. If anybody was in no position to patronize somebody, he was it. "Come on, Al, I'll back you up." A *smang*
of the strings. "No," I says, though they'd at least have
been able to *understand* me. It was a dream put by. Let
their last memory of me remain what it probably was,
on the stage of Southeast High belting out "How'm I
Doin' " as an *honest* bum, just dirty, not anti-antiseptic,
a tramp chalkmarking the alley gates for his fellows
who would come after, dressed in a handout coat and
a pair of frayed pants ill held up by a length of knotted
twine. I had a sudden urge to let this spook back me up
at that, while I showed them at least how the King's
English ought to be enunciated:

> *I may not be the best in town,*
> *But I'll be the best till the best comes round,*
> *How'm I doin'? hey, hey!*
> *Twee twee twee twa twa!*

But prudence won the day, the temptation to make a fool of myself passed. I would not make our Tut a queen beloved of a jester.

Then there were weeks when there weren't even any dates the like of that, when quail hunting was really slack, despite a goodly pocketful of Dupont's gift to the world, namely cellophane. One Sunday evening about nine o'clock I decides to call it another day at the monastery and drops into a neighborhood diner for a late snack before toddling on home. I sits down at a counter bay that's otherwise empty except for one young woman directly across from me, struggling with a club sandwich that's disintegrating in the manner of its kind. Head down, she darts me occasional glances to see whether I note her unladylike battle with extruding fragments of bacon and tomato, to say nothing of the colored toothpicks never intended by nature to rivet the likes of that together. Over my own coffee and sinkers I am gnawed by something familiar about her. Giving her the double-O, I sense she's trying to place me too. I'm watching her over the mug of java, blowing on it, when I tumble. Of course. It's my old high school teacher, Miss Piano. She taught me second-year French and also subbed for my English teacher toward the end of one semester. She seems to make the connection herself as she's sucking at her glass of Coke, because she begins to laugh with the straw in her lips, coughing and spluttering some. She dabs her mouth with the fragments of paper napkin left in her fingers.

"Albert Banghart."

24

"Miss Piano. You've cut your hair or something. Anyway you look younger."

"Thank you. What are you doing now, Albert?"

"Why, I'm with the Northrup Corporation."

"Oh, the hat factory. You're working there. My goodness, the last time I saw you you were on the stage at Southeast singing, 'How'm I doin'? hey hey! Twee twee twee twa twa!'"

"Yes," I smiled at the bittersweet memory. "I thought I wanted to be a singer once. I might have made it except for one thing." I dunked my doughnut and bit into it. "My voice. I really belong to the era of the big bands, I mean in my attitude. Of course now you don't need a beautiful voice. It's all gravelly stuff, and nobody's expected to catch the lyrics. Maybe I could make it as a rock singer. Sandpaper people's nerves."

"You haven't married?"

"No!"

"You sound positive. What's your objection to marriage?"

"The long hours."

"I see what you mean."

We seemed to be grooving, so I popped the last of the sinker into my mouth and carried my mug around to her side of the bay. I took the second seat away from her. "How about you? Still at Southeast High trying to teach them how to order french fries when in Paris?"

"No, I've been taking time out at the University to work on my master's thesis." She was chasing a piece of bacon around her plate in a way that made me doubt the truth of that. I don't know why except that I seemed to remember hearing that little Miss Piano had had a nervous breakdown and been in dry dock for a bit. She busily stirred coffee I saw was black, though I realize there may have been sugar in it. She shot me a smile over her shoulder as she hunched down to drink from the cup, pushing the Coke aside. It was the one shoulder her coat was hanging by. I tucked it around the other.

"What's the subject of your thesis?"

"Some translations of Racine, together with an introduction. Wasn't it your class I had read some of his plays? Even act out bits?"

The general trend of the conversation was such that your pinky began to lift of its own accord as you sipped your coffee — I had forgotten I could get it up any more. "I'm afraid my Racine is a little rusty," I said. "I haven't read any since then as I should." The waitress settled her butt against the side of the counter I had just vacated, nursing a toothpick as she watched and listened. It wasn't every day you got such intellectual fallout. "One has so much trouble keeping up with one's reading, don't you agree?"

Here Miss Piano swung away on her stool, choking. She was in stitches, shaking her head and licking mayonnaise from her fingers as with the other hand she tried to pull a fresh paper napkin from the dispenser. "I love club sandwiches, but they do leave you feeling you need a shower," she said, pretending to lay her hysterics at the door of that food.

26

I saw this number lathering herself in the stall, a phantom visible through the frosted door, working the suds into this, that and the other, a little of which I glimpsed down her blouse now as she bent to catch at her slipping napkin. A woman absolutely knows when she's being given the double-O there, and Miss Piano straightened abruptly, swimming into her coat with that backstroke they can never get right, and no man can help them with. I didn't want her to leave. I suddenly had the hots for her. Tie that! That's how slow business had been, and the five years' difference in our ages that obtained when I was a high school senior and she fresh out of college on her first teaching job, a gulf then, meant next to nothing now that we were both well into our twenties. When she flagged the neutral observer for the check, I moved to keep the conversational ball rolling.

"Funny what will stick in your mind. Know what I remember most about Racine? Your explanation about a *tirade.* You know — *teerahd.* These are long speeches every principal character gets at some point, to wrap up a whole lot of exposition about the story thus far and also give the audience a long hard look at him on his own. *It doesn't mean a chewing out.*"

Miss Piano doubled over in convulsions again. Was she a nervous case? She dropped a glove, thanked me in gasps for retrieving it, straightened a sleeve, all the while trying to pin her hilarity on her being so disorganized, not the other way around. Her agitation shook a smell of perfume from her person. "Have another cup of coffee. Miss," I summons the neutral observer, "two more."

"It's such a pleasure meeting up with a student after all these years who remembers something you told him," she said, finally composing herself.

That was what I thought. You spend your life trying to make truths sink in. Then what's so funny hearing them on other lips? Watching Miss Piano wipe her ripe-olive eyes with a handkerchief plucked out of her bag somewhere in the confusion, I says very slowly: *"Petit à petit l'oiseau fait son nid.* Little by little the bird builds his nest. The motto you taught us." This at least fell short of being a barrel of laughs, and, enormously encouraged, I leaned back, slinging an arm around the stool, and rocked my head and snapped my fingers as I sang:

> *How'm I doin'? hey, hey!*
> *Twee twee twee twa twa!*

I seized the moment some more. I lit two cigarettes and dragged away at both, inhaling deeply as I shook the match out and dropped it debonairly on the floor. Nothing. Both her and the neutral observer watched without expression as I chugged away at both gaspers. "Tell me, where are you living now? Do you ever hear anything of Miss Folsom now, our old English teacher? How are things on the Midway?" This was the first time the routine had ever laid an egg with a dilly or anyone else. Perhaps Miss Piano's face was a shade blanker

28

than the waitress's, still plying the toothpick as she stood watching. But it wasn't making a dime with either. I threw them a clue. "Paul Henreid and Bette Davis? In *Now, Voyager?*"

"Oh, yes, *now* I remember," said the waitress. "Then that's what you're doing."

"That's right."

Miss Piano still ne comprends pas.

"He smokes two cigarettes at a time?" she asks.

"No, no. He lights them for both of them, then hands her one. A romantic bit. 'Their' thing. Like this." I passed a gasper over to her.

"But I don't smoke."

"You want it?" I says to the neutral observer.

She looked hesitatingly around the diner. "I'm not supposed to smoke on duty."

"Well, hell, if —"

"Perhaps this once. I meant I was trying to quit," says Miss Piano, and, to cut the Gordian knot, accepts the fag. It's hard to think she ever had the habit, because when she puffs on it she holds it gingerly in her finger-tips, like it was the tail of a mouse. The thought stirs up other romantic associations of a private nature. "How about a brandy?" I suggest. "When we've finished our coffee and cigarettes."

Laughing fits are said sometimes to be repressed sex in the case of a woman. Or maybe she had the curse. I didn't remember her being prone to merriment in the old days. Or wait. There was one time she was so overcome with hysterics she had to leave the classroom for a few minutes. Some scholar had sat on a wad of chewing gum, and the sight of the fat lad pulling this seemingly endless cud off the seat of his pants proved too many for her — as it did to us too, so that didn't really count as symptom of any cracks in the plaster, though she was still boffing it up long after we had subsided. Through the glass top of the door we could see her trying to compose herself in the hall, wiping her eyes and tweaking her nose with a hanky. At last she returned, red-eyed and straightening her skirt.

"You've been working too hard on Racine," I said, now.

"Well, all right," she said, tucking this handkerchief back into her bag. "If you know a clean well-lighted place."

Having paid both checks I steered her around the corner to Feeley's. There she sat quite sedately in the booth, a complete and sudden contrast to what she'd been, as though she'd had her jollies for the time being, or was temporarily emptied of emotion, though for a moment she threatened to have another attack when I lifted my brandy and said, "Voilà!" Of course we rambled through a variety of subjects, among them the sexual revolution. I said I was for it, for anything that liberated the human spirit. "For it is the flesh that fuses two people into one living, breathing, meaningful whole," I says. "The body is sacred, don't you agree?"

She looked away dubiously, twirling the stem of her glass. "Well . . ."

"Because another thing I remember from your class,

this one was the English one you took over when Miss Folsom got sick? A teacher likes to think she's been an influence in a pupil's life, doesn't she? That she's molded his character?"

"What do you remember?" She looked wary.

"A line from a poem of John Donne's, that gives better expression to this sacredness of the body that I'm talking about than anything I almost read. 'Except you something me I never shall be free' — and this is it — 'or ever chaste except you ravish me.' "

"That's not what Donne means. That's from one of the Holy Sonnets, which begins, if you'll recall the whole thing, 'Batter my heart, three-personed God.' So it's a religious emotion he's expressing; precisely the reverse of a physical one, which he uses merely as a metaphor for divine possession. If anything he's renouncing fleshly lusts."

It struck me as rather petty to niggle over a thing like that, to split hairs when somebody's trying to groove. No wonder people can't communicate. All this lint-picking. Take this plate of cold cuts home, I told myself, hit the sack and call it cloister bells. I glanced at her glass to see how near empty it was, knocking my own back for a hint. I think she noticed. It was a sticky silence. I reached down to pull up my socks, which I could *feel fall,* cursing myself. Then I saw that she was watching me sideways, a glint in her eye and a faint trace of a smile on her thin, scarlet lips. "Have you ever heard the recording of Richard Burton reading Donne's love poems? I have it at home."

"Oh, you do? I'd love to hear it. I'll bet it's superbly rendered."

"It's a little late."

"Shoot, it's not late. It's hardly eleven." *Shoot?* That's right, Mac, you heard yourself. This is your old school-teacher, and crazy as it seems, those are her not-bad breasts resting on the table, like a meal waiting on a shelf.

She gave her head a toss, a habit seemingly dating from the days when she had a mane *to* fling back, the wealth of black hair since then cropped close around the sides and forehead like a Roman emperor's. And back-pedaled into her coat again. "I'll lend it to you to take home and play, if you'd like," she said as I came around to help her.

"Fine. And I'm conscientious about bringing things back." *Taking* them back, stupe. You take, she has it brought. "About returning things I borrow."

She lived as it turned out just around the corner, in a four-room flat on the third floor of an apartment building. I trudged up the stairs behind her, appreciating the calves and the ankles into which they tapered, perfect as baseball bats. I waited in the open doorway while she stooped with her coat still on to fish the love poems from a cabinet beside what looked like a swell hi-fi, itself near a couch as loaded with cushions as Cleopatra's must have been, on that barge that burned on the water like a somethinged throne.

"Are you sure you don't want to listen to a few with me now?" I said when she handed me the record.

32

"I think not. I don't feel in the mood tonight."

Develop that negative and you come up with nights when she must. I didn't have a phonograph, I was only taking the record as a pretext for seeing her again, in case this dry spell continued. I'd have to hear the poems first, of course, and so I rang up Faith Mullins, who I knew had a Magnavox, and made a date for the next evening. She was a bony girl with rather large teeth, and resorting to her showed how bad the drouth was. I regretted this date as I rang the doorbell to pick her up around seven — but not as much as I would. It was only when she opened the door to greet me, her smile blazing up between earrings much too long, that I revealed the record. "I thought we might play these later."

She took the record and looked at it. "Richard Burton reading — oh, my God — John Donne! Oh, *thank* you," she exclaimed, and gave me a grateful peck.

I was beginning to smell a little systematic confusion here, in fact things might be going to get a little cruddy what with the imminent possibility that I might never get this particular treasure back into the right hands again. I muttered something about my not having a phonograph, but what could that do toward straightening the mixup out? It made all the less likely my having any use for the record myself. "I can't wait to get home and play it," she said, with a little dance of anticipation. "I'll get my coat."

For I had dinner ahead of me too, before failing completely. After one of Feeley's famous steaks we went back to her place to listen. My recovery problem made it hard to concentrate on the complexities of John Donne. A bad scratch in the record gave me a bright pretext for getting it back. I told Faith as I was getting ready to leave that I wanted to exchange it for another. "No. I want to keep the one you brought me, Al Banghart," she said, hugging it, or rather the envelope it came in. It was one of those muddles there's no hope of getting straight. I had to leave empty-handed — and face Miss Piano that way too. Because not a shop on the South Side seemed to have a copy. But at least I had *heard* it.

"It's absolutely marvelous," I reported over the telephone. "Such a brilliant reading. I can't imagine anyone doing it better, or with a finer sympathy with the values of the original." Most of these comments were cribbed from Faith Mullins' dithers. In fact I had jotted them on a card which I was reading to Miss Piano over the blower. "A perfect union of two geniuses," I continued, holding it up to catch the light in the dim booth, "the one creative, the other interpretive. What a satisfying blend of skills, what a thrilling esthetic experience it all adds up to." I stuck the card in my pocket. "What are you doing tomorrow night? I feel I must repay you with at least a good dinner. We've loads to talk about. I forgot to tell you, Feeley used to know Yeats."

"Oh, I'm sorry, I'm busy tomorrow," Miss Piano said. "That is Saturday, isn't it? Sunday would be O.K."

I turned up with my Chevvy convertible washed and waxed, and my best suit cleaned and pressed — but mitout no record. "I feel I want to hear them again be-

34

fore I give it back to you, if I may. Do you mind?" I stalled.

"Not at all. You could keep it but for the fact that it's a present from a very dear friend. A cherished possession. Shall we have one drink here before faring forth? You look as though you could use one."

I watched from a window chair while she mixed us martinis, wearing a silk dress of a dark shade of blue that women with her swarthy coloring seem to find becoming. She carried my brimming glass to me like a picnicker in an egg race, then settled herself with her own drink with the same care in another part of the room.

"Voilà!" I said, lifting my cocktail.

"I hate to do this to you, but that's not a drinking salutation. You're probably thinking of 'A votre santé,' to your health. 'Voilà' is a sort of exclamation meaning 'There' or 'Behold.' "

In other words, another ball breaker, such as you didn't need the Women's Liberation literature on a nearby table to tell you. Nail the male, that was her cry whether so admitted or not. Constantly correcting your grammar, your opinions about life and letters, challenging you at every turn, it was all part of a pattern. I was glad Faith Mullins had the record. Who gave it to Miss Piano, some Lesbian? I hope Faith was stretched out right this minute, listening to Burton's "mellifluous snarl."

"What nationality are you?"

"My father is Italian, or was, and my mother equal parts French, Dutch, Scotch and Spanish," she said, as though giving you a recipe for a genetic dish you might care to try in another reincarnation. A regular eugenic treat. Now having asked for a drink of water I had the hose turned on me. She launched a detailed account of her parents' relationship to each other and hers to them. "It's so hard to think of our parents actually in love, much less in the physical conjunction that produced us. The whole thing is grotesque. You know? Their life together is prosaic by the time they get around to having us witness it. Still, my father would speak of their being deliriously happy. That was his phrase. It's impossible to imagine. They were always travelling — my mother's going around the world right now. She's going to make a long stopover in India, where they spent their honeymoon. One that nearly cancelled my reservation on this particular star, incidentally. Because he caught some Oriental fever and nearly died. At one point he had a temperature of a hundred and five."

"Maybe that was when he was deliriously happy."

"Yes, well it was touch and go, to hear them tell it."

So is this. But at least now we know the cure for those laughing jags. Just slip her a funny. Cool her down in nothing flat. Have her sober as a judge in jigtime. It's when you're serious that fractures her. Let's get this cheese *home*. Let's get this show on the *road*, so we can get her *back* home.

"Now you're admiring my ormolu clock. It's from

Naples, my father's birthplace. Another of my treasures. It's twenty minutes fast."

Christ, it's not even seven *thirty*? She's older than you, remember, you can always ask her what her feelings were when the Germans sank the *Lusitania*. Tell me, do you miss vaudeville?

"Tell me, do you still drive around in an open convertible wearing your cap with the peak switched around behind?"

"Let's go see."

"I remember you doing that from schooldays. I remember lots of things about lots of you. And I won't tease, because here we are . . . Where are we going for dinner?"

"I have a table at the El Conquistador. What's so funny? Oh, yes. I forgot. El means the. Redundant. It's like saying the L'Aiglon."

"No, I like it. The El Conquistador it is. I'll get my coat."

Gin went directly into her bloodstream. She sat with her head back in the car and her eyes closed, giving herself to the evening wind. And more reminiscence.

"You would prowl the neighborhood, combing it for girls I suppose. Your driving always had that prowling air about it; this cap on backwards, slouched down behind the wheel with a cigarette hanging from your lips, looking like a — You won't mind this?"

"I don't know yet. Say it and we'll see."

"Well, like a barnyard villain. You know, in one of

those animated cartoons? That dog or wolf who's always a menace to the other animals. It still lurks about the corners of your mouth, that up-to-no-good, ne'er-do-well something." She sighed. "Oh, I wish the El Conquistador were fifty miles away."

"Sorry, here we are."

I turned the heap over to a four-star general and we went in. Miss Piano wisely declined any more cocktails, contenting herself with the white wine I let her pick. Suddenly everything was changing. My spirits rose as we rapped about old times, as though we had both been students then. Early on in the meal I discovered something about her, or rather pinned something down I already had.

The off-and-on switches in her mood, the short-term swings and unpredictable reactions, had nothing to do with response or lack of it to what you were saying, or even to what she was saying, but were apparently emotional cycles going on inside her independent of the conversation. These seemed to have their own rotation times, determined by a sort of internal chemical clock. Either that or dictated by what she was privately thinking. We all have this scenario going on inside us, more or less tied to the one going on outside — more with some people, less with others, like Miss Piano, at least a good part of the time. Once she laughed when I told her my poor old grandmother thought people on television could see her and so never undressed in front of the set, and then nodded soberly (with slow sage blinks reminding me of Tut Carpenter) when I told her — this is a true story — about a woman I knew who, on learning that a rival hostess had a *bidet* in her bathroom, said she disapproved of hanging art there. She knew of some people who had a Corot in theirs, another couple with a Monet in theirs, and now here was this woman hanging a Bidet in the can. She thought it was the name of an artist. What the hell was Miss Piano thinking as she sat there nodding over her wineglass? Maybe something sad, and something funny the other time.

But when you meshed gears she could be fun. Two hours and twenty-five unregretted bucks later we were back at her place, where she dropped into a chair and threw her legs out with a glutted sigh. "That was wonderful. Fix yourself a drink, Al. Anything you want. Ah, without good food and drink, without these friendships — life, what *cauchemar!*"

"That means nightmare. I remember that from your class."

"But I'm quoting Eliot — did you learn that in Miss Folsom's?"

"There goes another testicle."

Because by now we were laughing together about all this sexual hostility stuff, making jokes about it. I settled down on the studio couch with some of the Women's Lib pamphlets earlier noted, getting her to migrate by asking questions about the contents that she could only answer intelligently by huddling over them with me. Charts and things.

"Does all this female business make you stiffen?" she asked.

"Part of me." Whoa boy, not so fast so soon. Easy does it. "I'm a feminist myself."

"How do you mean?"

"I believe in absolute equality. So take the aggressive. Invite me to stay the night, ask me to marry you, divorce me, then wind up paying the alimony so I can live happily ever after."

She smiled, settling her head back on two or three of the cushions of which there was this mountain on the couch. I leaned forward to toss the material back on the table, and when I sat back again it was to find her looking at me with those great dark eyes. She rolled her head away, running a hand through her hair. It was now or never, the deliciously perilous moment. To try to kiss her or not. I used an old trick. I finished my brandy and said, "Well, it's been most enjoyable," giving her a casual peck like someone saying good night, at the same time intending it as a reconnoitre. She looked straight at me without moving. I bent forward and pressed my lips onto hers. The scarlet thread was very responsive, and there was a nice clean taste about the mouth too. Sliding an arm under her shoulder, I felt her slip out of my grasp and onto her feet.

"Just not fair," she said, and turned off a few lights.

By the time she got back to the couch I was stretched out on it, a position in which she readily joined me. I bobbed at anchor for a while, then decided to send my tongue out on a probing patrol. It took a moment to coax her own from hiding. But when these two thrilling little conductors met, a fine electric current was set flowing between us. Once I felt her pink cathode withdraw, but only to pause a moment before slowly, tantalizingly travelling over my teeth. I sucked in my breath and said, "Well. Ask the French teacher about French kissing." She laughed and pummelled me a little with her fists. We were like school kids. It wasn't as though I had grown as much as she had youthened — if there is such a word, which I doubt. Anyhow, I figured now was the time to make my major move.

I had the customary sheet of cellophane folded and ready in my pocket. I had settled on the thick kind used around boxes of berries and things in the grocery store, which had produced the healthiest crackle of all those tested. Wrinkling it up under cover of a lot of spring-creaking racket I created by pretending to be shifting my position, I reached over the head-end and flipped the wad under the couch. The faint rustling began underneath us as the paper started slowly to unfold.

Miss Piano raised her head, cocking it alertly.

"What's that noise?"

"I believe —"

"Shh! Listen."

Silence. I thought this wad of ammo was finished. Then there was a last crackle.

She sat bolt upright.

"Mouse," she said, springing to her feet. "Here, quick, give me a hand. Damn place is full of them. Let's get this little bastard."

In a twinkling she had turned the lights on again and snatched a broom and a mop from a nearby closet.

"You get at that end," she said, thrusting the mop into my hand, "and I'll take this. When we pull the couch out he'll have to run one way or another. Get a good grip on it. Ready? O.K. — now!"

There was in fact a mouse, first time I ever ran into *that* complication, and when we yanked the couch away from the wall he scuttled in my direction with a suddenness that took me completely by surprise. Instead of bringing my mop down on it, I guess I kind of jumped out of the way, sort of maybe with a little startled exclamation, or outcry, or involuntary gasp. Miss Piano stood gaping at me. "Good God, what are you, a man or —" She caught herself midway this unfortunate ejaculation, now perhaps worse than if it had been blurted in full. Quickly recovering my presence of mind, I said, "Here, he ran this way. Let's get the sonofagun!"

But it was too late. I dashed into the next room, clattering my mop under chairs and tables, to no avail. When I saw Miss Piano putting the broom back into the closet I gave her the mop, which she stowed away too, without comment. I poured myself another brandy. It was one of those rotten breaks you get in moments when you're taken unaware, and try in vain to reconstruct later. When we sat down on the couch again we were two people in no mood to take up where they had left off. She leaned an elbow on the cushions, her head in her hand.

"Are you afraid of mice?"

"Good God no. It's just that I was taken by surprise. Completely."

"What do you mean? I told you what was there. What could be surprising about it?"

It was one of those situations the fastest way out of is straight through. There was nothing to do but come clean.

"I was trying to play a practical joke on you, Miss Piano. I dropped a wad of cellophane behind the couch. All right. When it unflexes, it sounds like a mouse. Or it can be mistaken for that. I was only trying to frighten you. So you'd want, like, protection?"

"I don't believe you. I refuse to believe the testimony of my senses."

"O.K., I'll show you. Get up."

She had moved the couch back against the wall. I pulled one end of it away again, far enough to reach down and retrieve the wad of cellophane, which I held out in my hand. "Hear?" I crinkled it in her ear by way of demonstration, laughing. "That cute? Just a little gag I thought might amuse you." I dropped it in an ashtray and shrugged. "So when a mouse actually did run out, my little jape backfiring, why, naturally I was taken unawares. That a scream? That most amusing?"

She was walking the floor with her arms folded, looking thoughtfully down, pacing with the deliberation I remembered from schooldays when she was determined to find the culprit responsible for some breach of the peace, like stealing the quiz questions or putting Limburger cheese on the radiator.

"You were quite sure the paper would perform as expected," she reviewed. "How did you know?"

43

"How did I know?" I asked in a dry voice. "How did I know what?"

"How did you know cellophane behaved like that unless you tried it before." She stopped and looked at me. "On other girls."

"On other girls?"

"For purposes other than to amuse." Her insights were uncanny. A woman's intuition at its most deadly. Her eyes X-rayed me. "This is the technique a dedicated lounge lizard uses to seduce girls. Putting to his own base purposes the moment when they cling to him for protection."

She let this sink in while continuing to fix me with her gaze — as I supposed she was, for I had dropped mine to the floor.

"Why would you think you'd need to resort to anything like that with me?" she asked, rather indignantly.

"You mean I could . . . ?"

"You certainly have a talent for making things worse and worse, don't you?"

"I guess. But I see myself as I really am, now. And I'll never do it again."

She ignored me, turning to the brandy bottle as she seemed to say to herself, "This is serious." She began shaking her head, pausing only long enough to take a gulp of the drink she poured herself. She left the bottle open for me to help myself to another, which I quickly did. Belting it back, I nervously eyed her walking the floor again, this time with another and even more sinister echo of carefree schooldays. It was the way, she

44

would let the class know, she took her time groping for the *mot juste* to describe something really hairy or kinky it or some member of it had done, in the line of either conduct or scholastic performance. There was the same sense of theatre in her deliberation now. At last she had the word to which birth must be given.

She made one more cross of the room, turned, and faced me.

"You're a poltroon."

"Yes, ma'am."

"Do you know what that means?"

"I have a rough idea. I'll look it up when I get home, but I know it's negative." These were bad vibes. I felt really lousy, realizing this was my moment of truth.

"This is the sleaziest, cheesiest thing I have ever heard of."

"I don't exactly like myself."

"Don't be smug. Let's lay everything on the table while we're at it, if that's agreeable to you. Bring it all out in the open. I've said we teachers know more about the students than they suspect, and a lot of things can probably be understood in the light of this."

"I don't expect to be spared anything, Miss Piano. Please continue."

"Very well, then. Did you not then belong to an organization who called themselves the Cherrypickers, for reasons obvious to anyone familiar with the argot of seduction?"

"We weren't a formal organization, like a boys' club with regular meetings or anything. Just a loosely knit

45

bunch of fellows with common interests. There was a gang on the other side of Stony Island that was much worse. They called themselves the Consumers Union."

"To rate the products tested I have no doubt, and later talk about them."

"That's not true. I would never repeat what happened here tonight."

"I can imagine that."

In a way I dreaded this dry tone more than the other, since it marked the third stage of her — well, *tirade*. Because she had taken in more of Racine's dramatic method than she probably realized. This stage consisted in summing up the action thus far in the form of a series of questions fired, not at you, or at herself, but as it were to an invisible third person, hovering there in the middle air. I believe it's the kind of speech known in English as an apostrophe.

"Can a decent, respectable human being be made of this," she said, flinging a hand vaguely in my direction without turning to look at me. "Can a mature person be constructed from these still adolescent — nay, possibly even juvenile — materials. *C'est la question.* Can bricks be made of this poor straw . . ." And so on. This speech was so effective I momentarily forgot it was me it was about, and listened with bated breath, awaiting the outcome that hung in the balance for this other unfortunate wretch, concerning whom so much was left to be desired, etc. But of course there was no "outcome" now. That all remained to be seen, in the future about which we were all so curious. There was no answer in the nature of the case, only this query mulled in a dazzling variety of ways, shapes and metaphors. Until the apostrophe, or *tirade,* ran its course, and the speaker plopped into the nearest chair.

By this time I had managed to pull my wits about me, long enough to pose a little question of my own. One that might find the chink in *her* armor.

"If you knew all that about me — and I'll say it was some dossier — how come you let me go as far as you did?"

"Oh, for God's sake, Albert Ernest Banghart. At least show enough of the maturity I've just been praying for to know the answer to that. I assumed that by the age of twenty-three, or whatever you are, you'd have begun to show at least the rudiments of a grown man. Maybe even a gentleman. Not think you needed gimmicks and stratagems to possess me. I mean nothing is more insulting to a woman than that."

That took what little wind was left out of my sails. It was my turn to walk the floor, stewing in my remorse. Beyond the window was a world of people who had earned the respect they enjoyed, free of the shame I had incurred. *Decent people.* They paid their bills and massaged their gums and went to P.T.A. meetings to fight budget cuts. They bicycled as a family. They had "our" songs, every last one of them, even if it was only *Barney Google.* They circulated petitions to spare scenic areas threatened by new highways for which they proposed more logical alternatives, alternatives which might pass the homes of corrupt officials whom they

47

then fought tooth and nail till they had won. They went without to educate children who themselves worked to supplement scholarship money with an industry for which the example had been set at home, and who when they graduated from college got into the corporations of their choice or joined the Peace Corps or signed on for arduous and even dangerous expeditions aimed at saving vanishing species. It was as though they all stood at their own windows now, this whole better element, some in nightgowns and even tassel caps, and faced me in silent rebuke, seeing me as Miss Piano did, who had made me see myself as I really was. What I experienced at that moment was nothing less than a spiritual rebirth. To redeem myself in the eyes of this woman became the one consuming passion of my life. But how? How could I ever even get to see her again, after this?

She supplied the solution herself without realizing it.

"A poltroon and a cad and a bounder," she was saying, as though taking it from the top again because there were a hundred *mots justes*, not just one. She sat inhaling one of my cigarettes as though she had never quit, blowing smoke out rather noisily through her lips and dropping the matchbox on the table end-over-end and picking it up again in rhythm to the epithets. "You're a knave and a lout and a churl."

"And a what?"

"Churl, churl."

"Oh, yes."

"A churl and a curmudgeon and a guttersnipe." It was

48

like having the Thesaurus read aloud to you, or recited from memory. "You're a rascal and a blackguard and a sonofabitch. You're a rake and a bastard and a scoundrel, and I want my record back."

Of course. That was the answer — to how I would get to see her again and start squaring myself. The record was the key to the situation.

But, of course, I would have to steal the damned thing.

3

I don't mean I broke into Faith Mullins' house. I just gave her a buzz next evening and asked whether I could drop around for an hour. I was in the mood for some poetry, of which she had recordings by the dozen. She said come ahead, and I popped in a little after eight.

"What would you like to hear, Al?" she asked, thumbing through the stack of LP's on the piano. "The cleaning woman puts them away all mixed up after I alphabetize them, my brother's jazz things in with mine and what not, but I can usually find what I want. Here, how about Gielgud reading Shakespeare?" I said that would be fine. Halfway through it she luckily got a phone call, and while she was talking in the next room I quickly snatched up the Donne-Burton which I had spotted earlier in the stack and secreted under the piano shawl, shot on tiptoe out the screen door and down the porch stairs, chucked it into my car and was back inside dreamily listening to Shakespeare when she returned. I called Miss Piano a couple of days later and she said it was all right to come by and bring the record that evening.

"I'd like to hear a little of it if I may," I said, when she let me in. "One last time?"

"All right, Albert, if you want," she said, her tone forgiving though still a little pedagogical. Maybe John Donne would exert a sweetening influence on us both, enabling us to let bygones be bygones. But when she set the LP on the turntable and started back to her chair, a blast of ragtime piano shattered the room, stopping her in her tracks. She took the record off and stared at it. "Who on earth is Knuckles O'Toole?"

"That damn cleaning woman," I said, gritting my teeth. "She gets things even more mixed up than I thought. I'll get this thing straightened out yet. I'm sorry. Do you mind if we listen to a little of this piano? It doesn't sound bad."

She shrugged. "What can we lose?"

She liked ragtime, as who doesn't in short bursts. She tapped her foot and rocked her head through *Canadian Capers* and *Ragtime Cowboy Joe*. But it remained for *Nola* to really stoke her up. She played it over two or three times. It was evidently a favorite. She swung her hands in rhythm to it, the ice cubes tinkling in her glass. Finally she hauled me to my feet to dance. "You waltz divinely," she said, "but this is a fox trot." She spun off alone while I watched from my chair, both of us beaming with pleasure. She lost an earring in orbit, which I looked for on all fours, in vain. An hour of music and dancing and drinking and she had quite forgotten the misunderstanding of the other night — enough for me to bring it up without too much embarrassment. I was surprised to hear myself. I told her she was a stage in my development, in that she had brought me up short and forced me to take a good hard look at myself. "Take inventory," I said. "I'd do anything to square myself with a woman like you. Even marry her, I mean if such a thing were in the cards."

Her smile was friendly, but it had just a twist of lemon in it. "Why should I get married," she said, "and give up my career?"

"I'd give up mine, if the circumstances were right. Hell, I don't have any talent, so what would I be giving up? I mean why shouldn't the man keep the damn house while the woman goes out to win the bread, *if* she has something on the ball? I'm just speaking in the abstract of course."

"Of course."

She was indifferent, which was a good sign — at least not hostile any more. I went on to describe my life as a constant quest for self-improvement, a policy of always trying to cultivate people a cut above myself, who were easy enough to find, alas, as we Bangharts were not the best of stock. Some progress had been made, though a lot remained to be done. I was not that boy who squatted behind billboards watching pedestrians try to pick up a quarter he had soldered to the sewer-grating, or even the young man of a somewhat later period pursuing the twofold ideal, of bagging his limit before getting married, and of staying single the rest of his life if possible.

"How long have you had this wish? To make something of yourself." She was on her own hands and knees, looking for the earring now.

"Ever since I was a boy, aware of the origins there was nothing to do but rise above." I helped her search, pulling chairs and tables aside as I dilated on a childhood with parents trying to rise above *their* stations, which often as not was each other. My father, who took the neighborhood wedding and graduation pictures, was rarely satisfied with the outcome of his shots, and would often call his customers back for a free sitting and another set of proofs — sometimes quite temperamentally summon entire bridal parties, forcing them to climb once again into full fig and on down to his studio if they wanted to see any finishes. His reputation was at stake. What did he care if the outfits were rented and the brother-in-law best man was back in Benton Harbor, it wasn't his problem. The dedicated artist sacrificed everyone to his craft, family, friends, only the creative outcome mattered. He wore a beret and chewed slippery elm to show that photography was an art form. And my mother? Never satisfied with *him*. He needed revision,

53

wasn't coming right. She was always on the lookout for something better, though nothing ever came of the affairs that were a kind of shopping for that superior masculine merchandise destined always to elude her. So everywhere this restless strain running through the family, this urge to find, to be, something better. "Why shouldn't I aim for a woman a cut above myself?" I finished this particular *tirade*. "How I would try to deserve her! I would plod, plod, plod for her." What was I *saying*? How far out of hand was this *getting*?

"Ah! There you are." Miss Piano reached under a magazine rack for the earring, which she rose and screwed on. She watched me as she did so. The fact that she had dressed up and was wearing jewelry suddenly seemed to me significant. That wouldn't have been necessary just to have a guy in the doghouse return a record.

The record. I told her she could keep the Knuckles O'Toole and meanwhile I'd try to find out what the cleaning woman had done with hers. All this while I'd had an order in for a copy of that with a local store, which now called to say it had arrived. I took that up to her the following week, removed from its envelope of course and wrapped in plain paper, so as not to add to the confusion — she already had an envelope.

Sipping some Chablis she had, we talked in the abstract again about marriage. I advanced the opinion that I didn't think the institution was toppling or even doomed just because it was no longer regarded as permanent. Here Miss Piano went into one of her characteristic (though maybe unconscious) tricks. She had a way of agreeing with you that left you with more egg on your face than if she disputed you. She did this by seizing the conversational ball and carrying it ten times farther down the field than you ever could have yourself, showing you, like, implications in your position you hadn't dreamt were there, till your own opinion seemed over your head.

"I couldn't agree with you more," she said. "I think there are a lot more instincts than are listed for us in the textbooks, and that some of these check, control, organize, even repress if you will, the ones familiar to us as expressing our basic animal nature. I call them counter-instincts. I mean domesticity is an instinct as well as the sex it moderates. It's universal in human life. It's inherent even in such a term as 'shack up,' which presumably puts sex at its lowest and most promiscuous. A girl today may have lain with as many boys as her mother kissed, but when she strikes one she really likes she'll do her damnedest to nail the relationship down, formalize it — for whatever length of time, as you say. Thus man so to speak controls, edits if you will, his Dionysian drives with the Apollonian half of his nature. What's that line from Wallace Stevens' poem, *The Idea of Order at Key West*? 'Oh, blessed rage for order, pale Ramon.' *Rage* for order. No, I couldn't agree with you more."

I nodded, not even able now to remember what the hell I'd said. I felt like an impostor, taking credit for all those findings, but there it was. I took a sip of my wine

55

and a bite of some Cheese Straws she had trotted out. "Speaking of Key West, I'd like to run down to Florida again. One of these days," I said. "Ever been there?"

She shook her head, her mind clearly not on Florida, even as a possibility.

"That's why your notion about getting married wasn't as wild as it sounded, however much you thought of it as coming out of left field," she said, setting her glass down on a table beside her. She gave me an oblique smile, or maybe sent it just past my left ear. "Were you really serious about being willing to look after a house for a woman with a career to worry about?"

"What would I be giving up?" I laughed. "A job in that hat factory!"

"Hm . . . It might just . . ."

"Don't give me your answer tonight," I said, my voice squeaking with fear. "Sleep on it."

"Let's both sleep on it."

She sprang to her feet, finished her wine standing up, took my hand and towed me into the bedroom. I drained my own glass en route, setting it down somewhere as we galloped on by.

She sat on the bed to take off her slippers and stockings. Undressing myself I saw her unzip her dress from the back with that act of contortion I supposed all single women had to develop and could forget once they had husbands to do them up or down. Maybe that was why some got married. Lightly dropping her brassiere and playfully kicking her pink pants into my face, she pulled

56

the covers back and stretched out on the bed with her hands laced under her head. I took her figure in hungrily. The breasts were full for a girl that small, as I already knew, as were her hips, the exclamation mark between blue-black, like her other hair. She watched me disrobe. When I was naked she dropped her eyes to my middle, then suddenly rolled over onto her side and buried her face in the pillow while the bed shook. More Smiling Through.

I stood at the foot-end, looking at her.

"You're a nervous case, aren't you?"

She flung around again onto her back. "It's just that that —"

"It's up to you to make it more impressive. And as for the pouch, that rough wrinkled look and all is probably what makes it resemble a frog."

"And accounts for the fairy tale about the prince!"

"Go to the head of the class."

"All right then. Hoppez-vous in . . . Hey, what about preliminaries? You know — foreplay?"

"Later."

It was quite good. So we became engaged. Then there was this long period of ducking into doorways and hightailing it around corners at her approach, hardly good courtship as I've admitted, but not fazing Miss Piano who filed it all away under Ambivalence, also already noted. There was something else in that period to which she did take exception however. It almost queered things, nearly crash-landed us on takeoff.

57

There was a crisis at the hat factory. The owners of this one-horse, but I think profitable, outfit sold out to a man named Gluckman. This buster left a lot to be desired, but where he really chewed out loud was in the area of human relations. He was no more than coronated Boss than, his eyes like bottle-caps, he tacked up a notice on the bulletin board saying that henceforth all employees must take the loyalty pledge. They must come up to snuff as patriots. I arrived one morning to find several of my colleagues clustered around it, in the short corridor leading from the office to the shop where I spent my days sewing bands on homburgs and snap-brims and porkpies. There were plenty of oaths, but none of allegiance. Still, nobody was willing to stand up to Gluckman. They were afraid for their jobs. They were scared.

"Well, I'm not," I says. "What are we — men or mice? This is a matter of principle. The principle of individual freedom. I know not what course others may take, but as for me, I'm going to tell Gluckman to go to hell."

They laughed, with a kind of nervous awe. "You'll lose your job, Al," Ernie Nelson said.

"Better than my self-respect. Better than knuckle under to a petty tyrant. I'd rather starve on my feet than live on my knees! This country has a heritage of —"

"Hold it. I think everyone should hear this." They all seemed to take courage from mine. I was lifted bodily onto a desk, the one used by the shop foreman, Pete Henshaw, who hadn't arrived yet. Nearly all thirty of the other employees had though, including the two girls who worked in the office. An old newspaper was slipped under my feet so I wouldn't soil Pete's blotter pad.

"My fellow Americans," I began. "This is a clear-cut issue of conscience. The clarion has called, the toxin sounded. Henceforth every man must examine in his own heart whether an employer has the right to twist his arm, and then decide, in the arena of right and wrong, good and evil, whether he is going to stand for it. This country has a heritage of freedom, paid for with the blood of others whose gift we have in sacred trust — the freedom to think and act without any pressure from self-appointed patriots. Of course we're all loyal Americans — loyal enough not to need the squeeze put on them by those with economic power over them! Now I ask you, my fellow Americans, would Washington and Jefferson stand for that blackmail?"

"No!" they all shouted as I pointed an arm at the bulletin board.

"Would Patrick Henry?"

"No!"

"Abraham Lincoln?"

"No!"

"Frances Parkinson Keyes?"

"No!"

I couldn't remember who that was exactly, and a doubt crossed my mind that it was the name of a founding father it sounded like. But their chorus of response lashed me to fresh oratorical frenzies.

"Then neither should we, inheritors of what they've passed on! The time has come to stand up to the fake

59

patriots and unthinking jingoists plastering the country with flag decals — like the author of that bulletin! What are they trying to prove? That they're more loyal than we are? Baloney! They're abusing our country's principles, leaving it to the rest of us to stick up for them. Stick up for them I shall with my dying breath!" A loud blast of cheers, with cries of "Attaboy, Al!" and "Pour it on!"

"That flag of ours, my fellow Americans," I continued, flourishing a finger in the air, "that flag was originally made for rebels. Now it's become a piece of pop art! Let's show these desecrators of our national emblem and these debauchers of our sacred heritage that we've got guts — the plain ordinary everyday guts — to stand up to them!"

There was a deafening roar. But those in the doorway looked behind them in a way that told me Gluckman had emerged from his office. The girls made room for him. He stood there in his shirtsleeves, the perpetual wet cigar in his hand, the perpetual clip fastening his tie to his shirt-fly over his paunch, the caricature of the Boss.

"Making a speech, Banghart?"

"Well, I was," I said, stepping down onto a chair and then the floor. "I think I'm finished now."

"So do I. Get your money. I think I heard enough to get the drift."

"Oh, you can understand English? I'm surprised to hear that. Then that leaves only one more thing for me to do. Ernie, would you tear that notice off the bulletin board and hand it to me, please?"

He sensed the parting gesture I wanted to make, and hesitated. He licked his rather buck teeth and smiled uncertainly. "Maybe we can compromise. Negotiate like."

"There is no negotiating with the Herman Gluckmans of this world. And certainly no compromising."

They stood away as I marched through the doorway back into the corridor where the bulletin board was, squeezing past Gluckman who remained as an obstacle. I yanked the notice from under the thumbtack holding it, tore it slowly into pieces, and dropped them into a refuse drum standing there. I spanked my hands together, gave my trousers a hoist, and walked out. At the far door I paused and turned.

"Don't let him buffalo you," I said. "If you all refuse to sign, what can he do? Nothing. He's not going to hire a whole new staff. The damn place would have to shut down for days, and losing even ten cents is more pain than he can bear, as you know. He can keep the few bucks I've got coming. Carry on!" And making the V for Victory sign I strode out.

The scene I left I can't vouch for in detail. Suffice it to say that several more walked out, and the next day all the rest in sympathy with their predecessors. My ringing challenge had borne fruit. My sacrifice had not been in vain. Not for nothing had I thrown down the gauntlet to a despot. There was a story about it in our community paper and one or two radio bulletins — the last being that Gluckman, faced with the paralysis of his business as a result of the walkout, gave in and revoked his demand. Everyone went back to work, except me.

I heard many compliments and comments from all sides — except from Miss Piano. Who you'd think would be the first to appreciate moral courage. But not a word. Finally I showed her a little editorial in *The South Sider* about how one man's unflinching integrity can be a source of inspiration to his wavering brothers, and by rallying the faint-hearted turn the tide in a crisis of spiritual decision.

"Did you see this?"

"Yes, I've been following it all closely." She was curled up in her stocking feet in a large chair, making notes from a history of French poetry. Which she now set aside. "I'm ashamed of you, Albert."

"Ashamed. She's ashamed of me. I put my neck on the line for principle, get my head lopped off, and she's ashamed of me." I saw how unconsciously I had adopted her method of firing apostrophes at unseen witnesses, to say nothing of the *tirade* for which we were both now deeply indebted to Racine. *"Ne comprends pas. Nix versteh.* Enlightenment, please? Why ashamed?"

"You were going to quit anyway. You were planning to leave the hat factory when we get married, so you had nothing to lose with your heroics."

"Heroics," I says, flinging up my hands. "I will not

play games with you. Games I can't play. I'm sorry. I'm not the type."

She went silently back to work. For a time there was no sound but a page turned and a pencil scratching on the legal pad resting on the arm of her chair. I sensed her mind wasn't on her work, and steeled myself for more *mots justes,* more and better apostrophes flung at sterner witnesses. Could anything be made of these poor materials, could a rounded-out human being result in the end, and so on. It turned out that she was still sifting out the facts in the case.

"Aren't you going to quit and run the house so I can take that job at Classic High? Isn't that the agreement?"

"The trial agreement? Sure. But it's six weeks till fall, and the money I was making would come in handy till then. But it's gone now, kaput. Dare to take a stand and they'll nail you to the barn door every time."

"Why aren't you going back and making an issue of it then?"

"What, and work for that slob? That petty fascist? I'll starve first. I'll get something. If worse comes to worst I can get my old job back as counterman. In the diner where we met? Did you know I was a waiter and fry cook there once? I remember those months vividly. Sixty bucks a week and unlimited Shredded Wheat. Or so it seemed, from the dagger looks you got from the boss every time you made your shift meal out of anything but cereal. You don't know what work is, you with your life of the mind, safe in your academic backwater, there. Not that I begrudge it. The sacrifices I'm willing to make don't stop at telling off the fat cats of this rotten world."

Miss Piano again set her work aside.

"There were people there who needed that job. You stirred them up to take a stand they had everything to lose from, you nothing. Playing the martyr entailed no risk whatsoever, so how do you expect any marks for nobility?"

"Here we go dishing out grades again. Who asked for them? My classroom days are over, so may I be spared report cards please?"

"But it's you who seemed to be asking for them, and I to decline."

"Please. No games. I said I was bad at them. So let's hear no more about heroics and martyrdom, let's not inject that element into something complex enough as it is. Oh, the confusion people can fling each other into in a twinkling! And as for arguing with women, trying to keep things straight and logical with them — huh! You blow such hot and cold a man wants to embrace you one minute and strangle you with one of your own stockings the next. Oh, what a mare's-nest life can be! What a tangle of inconsistencies we all are!"

"Far from homogeneous."

"Sez you."

"Am I to be crucified for agreeing with you?"

"Maybe. There are times when you treat me like — an associate!"

The upshot of this can be imagined, that we made love. One passion catches fire from another, proof of the very human unpredictability about which I had been ranting — I suppose that's not too strong a word. An hour's tumble in bed reduced us both to exhausted, reasonable creatures. Miss Piano saying she wasn't going to write me off: she was going ·to stick. To marry me. "Because the potential is there," she said, getting into her robe and slippers once again. "Which I know you can live up to, given half a chance. I know from experience that underachievers shouldn't ever be written off. There is that phenomenon, the late-bloomer, and it's true in the realm of character just as certainly as in the mental sphere. I said I'd marry you and I'll keep my part of the bargain. Because the potential is there."

We left it that way. Over a drink she got down her Shakespeare and read the opening of *A Midsummer Night's Dream*, taking all the parts herself. "Now, fair Hippolyta, our nuptial hour draws on apace . . ." But she still seemed preoccupied, troubled about something, and at last looked up from the book.

"What if Gluckman's bluff hadn't been called — as I'll grant you did call it. What if he didn't give in, stood his ground, and all those people were actually thrown out of work? Unemployment is up. They might not have gotten other jobs right away. It could have meant actual hardship for some of them. Their homes foreclosed, their children hungry."

"That was a risk I had to take," I said.

4

Rose Piano wanted to be married by a friend of hers, Shorty Hopwell, minister of a liberal church over near the lake front. That was how he was known not only to acquaintances but also to his parishioners. The bulletin board out front advertised the Sunday morning sermon, "Where Do We Go from Where?," by Reverend Shorty Hopwell. I thought as we entered the church to have the knot tied that evening that I'd like to have caught the 11 A.M., just to hear what certainties, if any, he could pull out of that morass of questions. But their specialty here was honest doubt.

Before performing the ceremony, he preached a short

sermon on the subject of marriage. His text was taken from a French writer named Quitard. "Marriage is like a beseiged fortress. Those inside are trying to get out while those on the outside are trying to get in." All this — the evening's message and our exchange of vows — was nicely integrated with the reading of a divorce form for another couple on hand who were calling it quits. For Modern Community had made divorce a sacrament, along with marriage, baptism and communion, in keeping with the aim to make religion relevant to all of life — "an institution to serve the whole man" was their slogan. The day before, there had been a sob-in, as some of the younger set called a funeral service, for a member who had passed on, so all in all it was a rich, full weekend for Shorty and his flock.

Shorty's position and the church's practices were often exaggerated in popular rumors, and I had personally buttonholed him to give him a chance to deny a story that he had agreed to a woman's request that at her funeral rice be thrown on her casket as the pallbearers ran down the church steps with it to the waiting hearse, on the ground that she was the bride of Christ now going to consummate that union. But Shorty said it was true. He defended any ceremonial that gave meaning and comfort to the individual. "What difference does it make as long as you don't believe any of it anyway?" he said. Officially declaring divorce a sacrament he defended on the basis of its being the second most important event in a person's life (or third, if you rank parenthood with marriage for the first two), as deserving of solemnization as the original vows. Maybe more. I couldn't quarrel with that.

"Dearly beloved," Shorty began, an impressively squat figure up there in his striped jeans and white turtleneck sweater, out of which the round face soared like a balloon tugging at its string, "we are gathered here to celebrate the flesh, both in the form of a pair being united in wedlock and in that separation reminding us that all things come to an end. This is a double ceremony of the kind we're not always lucky enough to have coinciding, to lend scope and balance to a Sunday evening. Which reminds me of a story about my grandfather.

"A horny old bastard, he used to greet me in the same way every time I went to visit him. 'Are you bangin' the dillies?' he would want to know. 'Are you laying plenty of pipe? Are you getting your cane varnished?' The conviction that there is pussy everywhere available, you see, dearly beloved, is important to these old goats. Well, I was in divinity school then and not gettin' much, as he would say, but I didn't want to do the old man out of his vicarious thrills, so I would always answer, 'Sure, Gramps, I'm laying plenty of pipe, I'm getting my cane varnished. I'm shucking my cob,' or whatever. Well, the old boy remarried at the age of eighty-four, and it was evident as the big day approached that he entertained grave doubts of a kind natural to a man that old marrying a woman twenty years his junior. They turned out to be groundless though. For after the honeymoon the bride testified to his stellar performance. He gave proof of his love nightly, sometimes two or three times. Even so he continued to mope and gripe. So we finally said, 'What are you complaining about? Three times in one night, a dozen times a week.' And he said, 'Yes — now that I'm too old to enjoy it.' ' "

I wondered what the unbelievers were doing tonight. I glanced around during the long yack Shorty's little parable drew, one that rattled the stained-glass windows. The church building, which had been bought from some bankrupt sect unable to swing with the times, had been remodelled into the form of a theatre, so that Shorty's sermon was being delivered from what was a stage. Drama was emphasized at Community as an art that had grown out of the church, to which it was now being given back (the way we talk about giving the country back to the Indians). It was a production of one of Rose's translations of Racine that had interested her in this congregation.

"The first of Christ's miracles," Shorty was saying, "alleged miracles," he amended with a sly grin, which fetched another boffola from the flock, "was the one at the marriage in Cana where he changed water into wine, thereby celebrating physical pleasure. But in actual fact marriage reverses this miracle. It changes wine to water. Right? Heh heh. The wine is all in the romance, from now on it's all water. Right? Heh heh. So that there is a kind of irony in Christ's alchemic gesture, bidding us eat, drink and be merry while we may. In this double ceremony tonight we unite two people still drinking the wine, and separate two others for whom it has turned to water. That is as it should be. We all know

69

marriage is for two people who want each other the worst way, heh heh . . ."

He knocked marriage a while longer, eventually returning to his text with the heartfelt wish that the two heading for Splitsville would manage to find their way successfully back into the beleaguered fortress with groovier partners, for another spell within its walls. I thought his message drug in places there, owing to the mixed metaphor it was laboring under I suppose, the fortress and the wine figures few speakers could juggle without a lot of hard breathing in the stretch. I snuck a look at the two calling it quits, and they seemed glad enough to be doing so, though determined to end matters with grace and go their ways amicably — which was one purpose and value of the new pioneering sacrament. It was frankly in a tryout stage, like a new show out of town, but so far it had had a hundred percent success. There had been no reconciliations. All the split-ups took.

The *pfft* sacrament was first, so that we might end on a note of triumph, or anyhow anticipation. The two stood up before the congregation while Shorty read a form that went "What God hath put asunder let no man seek to bind unduly." There was a double-ring ceremony, like ours, except that they were giving each other their rings back, no hard feelings. There were some other parallels with the knot-tying which then followed, the organ finally swelling into *Lohengrin* for fair. The ratio of dry eyes to moist was about the same for both, I'd judge, which probably spoke well for "the sense of life-reflecting symmetry" Shorty was driving at in the evening's combination.

Which now included communion.

This took the form of a regular church supper in the basement, rather than the traditional stiff formalization before an altar and so on, more of the flexible, realistic approach to faith. Hadn't the original Last Supper been an evening meal together? All right. Just as everything in life was a miracle, any repast shared was a form of communion. Any bottle of wine drunk together was a commemoration not only of the fellowship of those pouring it, but of the communion they, together, held with vineyards on a country hillside and the sun that ripened its grapes. Christianity had to be blended with the new Paganism if it was to survive, and that meant the mass should have its Bacchanalian side. Shorty even brought a touch of the connoisseur presiding over the eucharistic table (groaning with roast beef and potato salad prepared by the ladies of the parish to supplement the more meagre traditional fare). Swirling his glass under his nose, he sniffed the wine appreciatively a moment before remarking, "I think you'll find this a rather delightful little Beaujolais we're having our transubstantiation with. Good bouquet, and a certain claim to character that's modest without being apologetic." The bread was a crusty loaf flown in from France, but remarkably inexpensive. "Break and eat, I doubt whether you've ever tasted better." Chatting as we fell to now, he told us the case-price he got the wine for, always mindful of economy in the congregation's interest, and that got him to joking about how the groom was going to have to stretch his dollars from now on too. That got him on the subject of thrift, which reminded him of a story they told about George Jessel. It seems that, walking with a friend one time, Jessel saw a sign reading "Jesus Saves," and exclaimed, "Not like Cantor." I admired the mileage they got out of this new religion there. They got everything out of it. After this there was nothing left but devil worship. All in all, a splendid "last supper" for the divorcees, as well as a wedding feast to remember for the newlyweds.

But something was bothering Shorty you could tell.

It was the failure of the church's musical director to show up. He had promised to compose an original prothalamium for the occasion, and Shorty was irked by his tardiness, or absence for all we knew, because this new appointee was notoriously unreliable about dates and times, living in another world as he did. But at last Shorty's face lit up at the sight of something coming in the basement door. A smattering of applause for the event made me turn around in my chair to see.

It was a figure in a bright but shapeless mod getup, with hair that hung to his shoulders and half obscured his face, clutching a guitar case. He made me think of the ending of a poem by Yeats, *The Second Coming,* that Rose was so mad about she read it aloud often enough for me to have practically learned it by heart. Head ducking forward under the tangled locks, a tooth missing from his grin, he put me in mind of that "rough beast, its hour come round at last," that "slouches towards Bethlehem to be born." He took the guitar from its case, slung the instrument around his neck, and came forward. It was then that I recognized The Stopped Up Sink. He was in charge of the rock music featured here. He froze in his tracks when he saw who I was. We exchanged looks of mutual horror, then he came up to shake my hand and be introduced to the bride. He apologized for his lateness, explaining that he had been entertaining a sick parishioner. Then with the familiar violent *twang* of the guitar strings he launched into the prothalamium he had composed:

See ya gonna gotcha frucks
Alla wella muncha grucks
   Even as the teedy oh hay . . ay . . ay!
While ya twickle on the branks
May the moonlight bless ya ganks
   No matter what they teedle . . um . . day!

Oh, potato makes it quizzle
But don't yever let it drizzle
   On that two-by-two para . . hay . . hade!
Getcha groovin' with ya glands
Till Tuscaloosa understands
   Then you really got it may . . hay . . hade!

I jumped to my feet and shook his hand when he finished.

"Gee, thanks, Stop," I said. "I know you've done enough, but I wonder if Rose and I could have a copy of that."

73

"I never put things on paper," he said, "but I'll tell you what I'll do. I'll cut a platter and send you two a copy for a souvenir."

Which left us as much in the dark as ever about the lyrics. We would never know what he had said, or hoped, or celebrated, for us.

After that we trooped back upstairs to the main auditorium for a short production by the church's drama department. It was in the current mode of audience-participation theatre, a free-swinging work full of inflammatory outcries and general abuse of those out front by cast members who finally poured off the stage and up the aisles shaking their fists, shouting threats and taunting us to get *involved,* not just sit there with our mouths full of teeth, mere bystanders. The idea, as it began to boil up into a climax, was that we should take sides (in some abstract question never specified), and mix it up with them in a simulated street melée. Not so simulated either in the end. It was touch and go whether we'd all wind up with our mouths quite so full of teeth as we started. I tried to belt the male lead, purely in self-defense, but he hung one on me first. Then one of the placards wielded by a feature player came down on my noggin, laying a small section of it open on the left side. Nothing much, but there was a trickle of blood calling for first aid from a kit, fortunately one of the props in the piece. As I laid there on the floor having iodine dabbed on it by one of the better-bosomed picket-line Bacchantes, wishing this wedding night would never end, it occurred to me that I was

74

probably cheating the congregation out of the one thing that would have made the evening complete as a meaningful spiritual experience — a last rite scene. How they could have shown the church ministering to the whole man, if my wounds had only been mortal! But they were all good-natured about it, laughing sympathetically down as I was being touched up by the dish. Shorty's moonface beamed out of the circle. "You were superb, Al," he said. "You're a brilliant theatre-goer."

"Thanks," I said. "But, of course, what I really want to do is direct."

5

Morning of a fine day in mid-September. Rose is off teaching at Classic High, a private school near our apartment, which is the bottom floor of a three-flat just west of Stony Island. I have kept my promise to run the house, leaving Rose free to pursue her career. I'm holding up my end of the bargain on all that. Relishing the glorious weather, the spanking breeze, the spring of the still-green grass underfoot, I run a damp cloth over the clothesline in the backyard, preparatory to hanging out my wash.

I was pinning some things on the line when I happened to glance over and saw the woman next door doing the same thing. We'd nodded before, but now she seemed to drift tentatively toward the fence from between rows of flapping shirts, and I stepped around my basket to join her there, thinking as I did so: And there are women who want to leave all this behind to take jobs in offices and factories, in the name of emancipation. I shook my head in disbelief.

"I see you prefer this too," she said, smiling over the fence. "To drying machines."

"You bet. I think it purifies the clothes to get the sunshine, in a way that mechanical contraptions never can."

"It's much more hygienic than a dryer. My husband, George, is just as much a nut on the subject as I am. Natural is always better, whether it's food or anything else. 'Rochelle,' he says, 'there's vitamin D in the sun you'll never get anywhere else.' Of course he's preaching to the converted."

"Here too. I feel we pay a price for progress."

"For progress," she said, nodding along, in that way women have of echoing what you've said. "We gain a lot in convenience with machinery, but it's not the whole story."

"Not the whole story," I said, fascinated with this conversational technique. "The wash machine is as far as I'll go — not that we've got the money for a dryer just now. I felt the wash machine was all we could afford at this stage. But look at those things flapping in the wind," I said, gesturing to her line and mine. "It's poetry. It even looks healthy."

77

"That's the way George feels. 'Rochelle,' he says, 'you can blindfold me, and I can tell whether a shirt I'm putting on was sun-dried or spun-dried.' "

I doubted whether I wanted to hear any more of George's *bon mots,* even filtered through those ruby lips. She smiled continually as she talked, teeth flashing as white as her bedsheets. She looked to be pushing forty, and correspondingly well-upholstered, but appetizingly so, a peach not quite overripe, dripping with natural juices when bitten into . . . "You look as well as sound like a commercial for the sun," I said.

"As a matter of fact I am a sun worshipper," she laughed, and gestured at a patio on which were a rubber mattress, some lounge chairs, and a low table with a transistor radio and tanning lotion on it. Then she nodded at my line and asked a question I could hardly believe. "Tell me, how do you get your wash so white?"

"I use Swish," I said, "now with improved enzyme power. I never have to pre-soak." I didn't hold a box out for my pitch only because I didn't have one there. "Why don't you try it, and say goodbye to dingy drawers and stubborn stains."

Her face clouded. "I can't. My husband works for another leading detergent. He's district sales manager for it."

"Oh, he's a district sales manager? Does he travel a lot?"

She sighed, her breasts heaving under her blue jersey. "He's gone a good half of the time."

We had many a pleasant chat over the fence, especially after I adopted a policy of doing a little wash every day instead of letting it pile up into a mountain giving me the Monday morning blahs. A peek over its rim would generally find her stretched out in the sun in her bikini, confirming what I had already deduced from the drift of radio music. When my head materialized there with a cheerful "Good morning" she would respond with an invariable "Oh, hi," hitching up her halter and then extending a plump arm to turn the transistor down. She was a nut for Hawaiian music, whose constant woozy strains tended to give me *mal de mer*. It may have been one reason why Landgrabber, which was their name, was a confirmed road runner. Lusciously plump, as I've said, she looked as though she and the rubber mattress on which she lolled had been blown up together until they had both reached the desired proportions. A man in his own good health couldn't help noting the corrugated raft was double-bed size.

I don't know where the idea ever got started that a woman's work is never done. Mine was always done by noon, at which time my thoughts would turn to the pneumatic dilly next door, who didn't seem to have any at *all* aside from the washing. A day with the least hint of sun, or even promise of it in this waning summer's end, would find her on the air mattress or sitting in a lounge chair with a reflector held up to her face, her eyes closed in prayer to the blazing god. I could see her from the kitchen window, I learned, if I stood on tiptoe on a chair and peered down from one corner of the upper pane, holding the curtain aside and seething with the sexual frustration that is the lot of civilized man. Pretexts for conversation sometimes ran as thin as wash in need of being done. One morning I strolled to the fence after hanging out three handkerchiefs and a dishtowel.

"Have you read where Congress passed that appropriations bill?"

"They're always passing those. George says deficit spending has got to stop."

"Where is he now?"

"Omaha. This is no life," she purred contentedly, buttering her arms.

"Oh, tell me," I says, the straight man in this commercial, "what kind of lotion is that you're using? The results are certainly divine on you. I certainly envy you that tan."

I had seen George, and he didn't look like much in the way of competition. He was carrying the garbage out to the alley in his shirtsleeves, a rite in which no man is at his best. He had a slight pot that I thought harmed his cause, and his taste in clothes would hardly recommend him to the ladies if what he was wearing at the time was any gauge — mustard-colored pants that you hoped for his sake were not part of a suit, a matching shirt with the cuffs rolled up three turns, and one of those white cloth caps with transparent green peaks, like an old book-keeper's eyeshade. He walked very erect, as though he had been marching in a parade he had got separated from. I experienced the slight physical shock a man feels in the presence of a sexual rival.

These reflections cost me the name of Mrs. Land-grabber's lotion, though I did hear her say it let through tanning rays while filtering out harmful ones. "I'll let you in on a little secret of my own," she then went on. "To get really dark, mix a few drops of iodine in with the liquid." I wondered whether I might borrow her bottle, even this late in the season. "Sure. Catch." I naturally missed, letting it drop just inside her yard. "Please don't get up," I said. "I'll get it." But she was on her way over before I could jump the fence, tucking up the dumplings I had so often in fancy stuffed my mouth with. She fished the bottle out of a clump of hollyhocks and handed it to me. There was nothing to do but oil myself and stretch out, stripped to the waist, in a lounge chair in my own yard. The sun went in five minutes later and so did she, leaving me to sit there reviewing my position.

Housework may be stifling to the spirit, but a woman's place is in the home (a) unless she has more on the ball than me and (b) as long as she has a husband serving a life sentence in an office or factory because he once thought he saw a flash of heaven in the blue of her eyes. There are just as many men stuck in offices who'd like to write as there are women stuck in kitchens who'd rather dance — or work in an office! But they aren't taking to the streets demanding release from mortgage and millinery bills, much less have a lobby going for them in the form of Sunday-supplement anthropologists explaining their Ordeal. Which so much for male chauvinism. What's so stifling about housework that isn't about running a punch-press or bagging your monthly quota in Sales? Or even if it is, what's so soul-suffocating about it that you can't stand for a few hours before popping off to lunch with the other girls? My chores took so little time I began looking for ways to prolong them, as well as add a bit of amusement. For a while I went through a game of dusting with my eyes closed, feeling my way carefully along table-tops and around bric-à-brac. Then there were a few days when I made the beds with my feet. This meant getting down on the floor on my back and stuffing in the covers with my heels and toes. To tuck in the "hospital corners" I would lift the mattress with the heel of one stocking-foot and shove in the sheet with the toe of the other. This entailed a lot of wriggling and grunting around the bedroom floor, but I didn't mind; arduous though it was, I wasn't complaining; it beat working from nine to five at the hat factory, the very thought of which made me groan out loud. Yet that is what lots of women seem to want — even "demand" — and more power to them. I for my part wasn't complaining, full of self-pity.

Another way I had of beguiling the time was to imagine I was married to a different person altogether each day. I made my morning's selection very early from *A Treasury of Great Women* that Miss Piano had kept from her grandfather's library for sentimental reasons, and then spent an hour or so boning up on that particular spouse in order to be an ideal husband to her, sharing her ideas and hopes and dreams and so on. Among those I pretended would come home through that door to me at eventide were: Ella Wheeler Wilcox, Carrie Jacobs Bond (author of *A Perfect Day, Just A-Wearyin' for You* and other heartfelt songs), Margaret Fuller and Mrs. Pankhurst. There was a helpmeet, that Mrs. Pankhurst! Mr. Pankhurst too was an ardent suffragist, and what else? Nothing she ate would ever have dared to disagree with her. She popularized the woman's cause by breaking windows, pouring acid into mailboxes and burning buildings. Not that I blamed anyone who did (the world is of course paradise today because they got the vote) but the job I had comforting some of these warriors come nightfall! The heads I must take to this breast! There, there, baby, not so bellicose now, eh, relax over this bite of supper I have ready for you, nothing much, just pheasant under glass and a bottle of white Burgundy, topped off with this here raspberry glacée, after which we'll hit the sack and give poor tired hard-working baby a nice beef injection, there, that better? She yields, exhales a long blissful Ahhhh!, she is one smitten kitten. Lydia Pinkham and Mathilde Wesendonk (Wagner's mistress) were among my other selections, though they weren't in the treasury of notable female parties.

I was trying to work things out with George Sand and damn glad I was only dreaming (Henry James hit the nail on the head when he said she might have been a man but she was no gentleman) when the blow fell. Mrs. Landgrabber painted. So having to look at her work would be the price-tag on any ripening of this acquaintance. It ripened elsewhere than in the backyard, where a woman would naturally resist being wooed while looking like a channel swimmer. Here is what gave.

Until the weather turned cold, or unless it was bad, the neighborhood dillies would all straggle out of their houses shortly after noon and congregate on the steps and stone fence around a large apartment building across the street, to chew the rag. Some would rock babies in prams, a few would take a little knitting or needlework, but mostly we would chin. I say "we" because I soon took to joining them, as did a couple of retired gents living on the block, who would roost among them in shirtsleeves or those cardigans elderly men seem to fancy for some reason, sucking on their pipes and pulling up their socks. The klatsch would begin to break up when the first of the school-age children came romping home, but until then we'd sit and gossip the sunny hours away. One day I was pleased by the sight of Mrs. Landgrabber crossing the street to join us, freshly groomed in a flowery cotton print. She knew most of the crowd, and I introduced her to the rest. The talk continued its usual rambling course, winding around to the inevitable question — what to have for dinner that night. And didn't we all groan in chorus at the thought.

"Know what I think I'll have tonight?" said a thin, pale woman named Mrs. Bowser, who always sat at the far edge of the group, huddled over herself. She had the biggest wardrobe of what looked like hand-me-down clothes I have ever seen. Or maybe it was just that she never threw anything away herself. Anyhow there she was: never the same dress twice, and each drabber than the last. She always seemed to be talking to herself, even when addressing a subject of general interest. "I think I'll fix chicken alla cacciatore."

"I think it's chicken cacciatore," said another woman, rocking her pram by the handle. "The à la would make it French, and I believe it's Italian. Isn't that so, Al?" This was directed to me as one whose wife was half Italian, but before I could answer Mrs. Bowser cut testily in, yet at the same time as though muttering to herself, "I said alla, not à la. There's an Italian alla, one word, not two. A-double-l-a. Pronounced like the prophet Allah. You see it that way on menus sometimes."

"I think without it is preferred," the other woman persisted. "Just chicken cacciatore."

"Anyway it is Italian," I said. "Cacciatore means hunter. So it's a hunter's dish. Hearty."

"You mean they're out shooting deer all day, these men, and come home and eat chicken," Mrs. Bowser ran on in her nasal tone to no one in particular. "That's a hunter's dish."

Rochelle Landgrabber chimed in here. "Anyway I wish I could fix it. I've always wanted to be able to fix interesting dishes like that, but I've never learned to cook. I mean really. Too busy with my painting, I guess."

"They're out hunting deer and wild boar in the woods all day, these hearty men, and come home to a meal of chicken. That's where it gets its name," Mrs. Bowser went on. She worried a grievance the way a dog worries

85

a bone. I little dreamt I was about to fall into this woman's clutches, in a train of circumstances beginning right there and then.

"Anyway, I can fix that dish," I said, "and am ready to teach anyone else how." I laughed in the direction of Mrs. Landgrabber, who smiled and raised her eyebrows. "Any day."

It isn't really very complicated to make, and we had a skillet of it simmering in her kitchen by early afternoon two days later, ready for the Landgrabbers' dinner.

"Now I'll show you my paintings," Mrs. Landgrabber said, the reward I was hoping we could skip after piping one or two suspicious-looking daubs on the walls. They were hung all over the house, a tour of which was hence involved.

I don't think paintings have to "look" like something — but neither should they resemble the glops on the artist's palette. As these did. "I have never seen anything quite like them," I said, and "This one is really unusual." Eventually I was reduced to exclamations as shapeless as what I was praising. "Now, this is one I recently finished," she said, leading the way into the bathroom. We stood among fixtures rigged out in matching fabrics, right down to the clothes hamper, viewing a foot-square canvas framed in gold. I want to look at paintings. I don't want to look at paint. Which is what I mean by color arrangements that have made no progress from the lumps of pigment they originally were on the artist's mortarboard, like those musical compositions that are indistinguishable from the orchestra tuning up to play them. This one was typical of a new period in which Mrs. Landgrabber squeezed paint directly from the tube onto the canvas, in very thick layers. "Makes me want to reach out and touch it," I said. Inhaling at such close quarters a perfume that anesthetized the reason, I hears myself babbling in addition, "As I do the artist. In that dress." She laughed and said, "Maybe I'll make you take a cold shower."

"If you'll take one with me."

"You never know."

She led me off to show me her scrapbook. Sitting side by side on a couch turning the pages into which were pasted notices of some of her shows in cities where she had previously lived, such as Omaha, Gary and Peoria, our hands occasionally grazed, firing my blood. She made no more effort to avoid these contacts than I did — which raised my hopes that business could be done. When I made the first ticklish, critical move toward tentatively stroking a finger with one of mine, she clapped the book shut, sprang to her feet and said, "Come on. You've been a good boy letting me bore you with all this and I'll fix you some coffee. I always have some in the middle of the afternoon. Like the British with their tea. How about you?"

"I'd love some."

I sat at the kitchen table watching her brew it with an egg, an art almost lost. The result was delicious. How cozy this was, how ideal my marriage was for a man with this strong domestic side.

"Oh. How about a doughnut," she said, and in a moment a familiar and provocative sound made me prick up my ears.

It was the cellophane wrapper she was tearing open on a fresh box of doughnuts. It crackled with a tantalizing reminder of old days. I stared at it lying there on the table between us, still half around the box, fighting the temptation that threatened to seize me, now that I suddenly realized how far I had backslid even in coming here. There was a peculiar wrench of emotion in being egged on by something that at the same time brought me up short. Gave me unexpectedly the means of furthering my designs while showing me they were nefarious. My temptation was my rebuke, and vice versa. It made me see, for what it really was, the intention into which I had unconsciously slipped, and in so doing summoned up my better side.

For how long? That was the question. The reprobate in me struggled with the reformed husband. For a while it was touch and go. Then with a surge of lust let loose by another whiff of that nose candy and a demolishing glimpse of that lurking bosom the reprobate began slowly, inch by inch, to win this unequal tug of war. Inch by inch, the reformed husband gave ground. The sight of Mrs. Landgrabber walking to the stove for the coffee pot to refill our cups made it a full rout. Under cover of a lot of coughing and chair scraping, I snatched the wrapper off the doughnut box and wadded it up into a tight ball. I had it in my fist as she toddled back with the pot, jiggling in every contour, her flesh dancing under that orange dress. Mesmerized, I watched the coffee cascade into our cups. When she walked to the stove again I moved my fist around behind my chair and, laden with remorse, flipped the wad into a corner.

"What's that noise?" she said, starting to sit down but catching herself.

"I think it's a mouse. I just heard it a minute ago too."

"Oh, my God!" she shrieked. "I can't stand those things! I have an absolute thing . . ." She was standing beside me, an arm already around my shoulder as I rose to put mine protectively around her. "There, there . . ."

"Oh, my God . . . What are we . . . ? Al."

"Rochelle."

"I never do this."

"I know. We can't fight it. It's no use. We're drawn to each other. A harbor from the storms of life, the tense international situation . . . I don't know."

After the long first embrace we drew back and "gazed at each other with a wild surmise," like those lovers of old poesy, high — how does it go again? — high on a peak in Darien.

The honeymoon being over consisted, for Rose, not in disillusionment with me, but over the "arrangement." Her delight in our life-style, so keen at first, dwindled as the months went by, finally ending in open complaint.

"I think you should get a job," she said one evening, after an hour of glum silence that climaxed a week of deteriorating mood, during which I wondered worriedly what was eating her. "I mean I don't like this." She gestured around the spotless apartment. "It's not natural. Me working all day and you running the house."

"What difference does it make as long as we have a going concern? And who'd cook the meals and keep the place clean while I was out? We'd both come home to a dirty house with no dinner waiting. How could that be better?"

"We can hire a cleaning woman and eat our meals out."

I shook my head dubiously. "I don't know. The expense of that would probably exceed what I made. You know what restaurant dinners cost — and as for what cleaning women get an hour! No, don't knock this arrangement. *I'm* satisfied."

"But I'm not."

"Why not? We wanted to strike a blow for equality —"

"Oh, for God's sake, Al, stop talking about striking blows for things. And take off that ridiculous apron."

"This is a bottle-washer's rig from my diner days. To which I suppose you want me to go back! No, siree. Thank you just the same, ma'am."

"You wouldn't have to go back to the diner — or even the hat factory. You could get a job in an office."

"I don't want a job in an office. They're soul-stifling." I stood in the middle of the living room with my hands spread. "Look, this is what you wanted, why complain now that you've got it?"

"Well, I don't want it now! I've changed my mind. I sense people smiling behind my back, even the ones at school who first congratulated me on getting such an ideal husband in terms of the circumstances. A brilliant catch. Huh! They're jokes, like the wisecracks the drug-store cowboys don't even wait to make behind my back. 'I guess we know who wears the pants in that family.' And 'Wonder what he feeds her for breakfast — probably milk toast.' And they're right. It's not natural, really. It's against nature."

"Oh, it's nature is it now. Well, you asked for it. You're the sex who want the tables turned."

"Not this turned. Do you know you're called Mr. Piano? That's more advantage than I want, and should be more disadvantage than a man wants. He shouldn't be doing a woman's work."

"Aha! It's out. The whole Women's Lib case lies in smithereens at our feet. Men and women *are* different."

"All right! We're different. Don't crucify me for changing my mind. Or modifying my position. A woman wants equality with a man, but she wants a *man*. Not a . . ." She seemed to bridle at a word in her mind, at which my radar made a guess. It wasn't mouse any more, now. It was something else.

"Not a what? Parasite?"

"I didn't say that."

"But you thought something at which you shied. What was it? Not saying? That means it was something worse, so we can settle for that. I don't mind another *mot juste*, but I wish they wouldn't keep changing."

"The circumstances keep changing, and with them the words — with which we strive to make this paltry converse!" she added, suddenly flinging ten fingers into the air in a fit of Latin ancestry.

I smiled patiently. "You needn't take a pedagogical tone with me, my dear. It's eight years since I flunked French."

This seemed to empty everyone's quiver for the moment. She lit one of her few cigarettes, punching it out after a few drags, but thoughtfully. "There's something else I wonder about," she said after a moment. "What on earth do you find to do all day?"

"Oh, I keep busy." I laughed. "You know what they say about a woman's work. It's never done. You can imagine it takes longer with a man doing it!"

"No, seriously. What do you do? Like afternoons. Anything but sit out there on the fence yacking with those women? You're always out there any day I get home early."

"We don't just yack."

"What else do you do?"

I lit a cigarette myself now. I drew on it slowly as I paced, looking thoughtfully down at the floor. "Tell me," I said, "how long have you had this idea that people are talking behind your back?"

"*Mis*ter Albert Banghart!"

She was out of the parlor and into the bedroom like a tornado, the door slamming behind her like a pistol shot. I finished the gasper, sat for another half-hour with a highball, and went in. She was sitting up in bed painting her nails.

"You mean there's a word for that sort of thing?" she

said, her dark eyes flashing. "Is that what you've come in here to tell me?"

"We'll compromise," I said. "I'll look for part-*time* work. How does that strike you?"

She dipped the brush into the polish and silently decorated a thumb.

"No more fry cook jobs though," I laughed. "That's where I learned the basics, that stand me in such good stead now in the kitchen, but I've had enough of that. Maybe I could get work with that cleaning service Mrs. Cantwell was telling us about the other day. Several people on the block here use them. They send men to clean a house from stem to stern, which rather spikes your what-do-you-call-it, *canard,* that housework is only for women. Big strapping bruisers come in and *dust.* Isn't that rich? Char*men,* hey?"

She screwed the cap back on the bottle with gingerly fingers and swivelled out of the bed. "So I've got a persecution complex."

"Now it's my turn to say I never said that."

"You implied it."

"You needn't get paranoid about it."

"There, you said it."

"Oh, for Christ sake! This is the screwiest argument I've ever heard of in my whole life. I was only raising a point that seemed logical at the moment. I was concerned."

"Oh, so now you're concerned. So am I! As I've been trying to drum into that —" She looked at the cranial concrete in question, in a way that amply substituted for the word we were boggling at this time. She sliced the air with a sigh. "There's a — hazard to my self-respect, my female self-respect if you will, which you ought to try to understand. I don't want to be thought a woman who enslaves a man, much less enjoys doing so, which becomes the inevitable corollary of that."

"But I don't feel enslaved. I've never felt freer, believe me. You women want —"

She stamped her heel. "Damn it, will you listen to me! I don't want to be thought by friends and neighbors an Amazon castrater."

I turned away, my shoulders hunched. "I don't know what's happened to us. You used to laugh at me . . ." I shook my head. "I like this life."

"I don't! And I want you to go out and get a job. If you don't I'll —"

"You'll what?"

"I'll get a divorce! Anything but this — this feeling I have that people think I'm married to a man without starch, no lead in his pencil, no balls, call it anything you want."

"So it's what people think that matters, not what you yourself know in your heart of hearts, your deepmost self —"

"It's what they think of you. We all have to live in the world, which is such a complex and subtle tissue of reality and illusion, such an insanely delicate balance of fact and imagination, of —"

I never heard what else it's an insanely delicate balance of. The doorbell rang just then and when I went to answer it there was Mrs. Bowser standing on the porch. The one who put up the argument about chicken cacciatore. She was drumming up contributions for — I don't remember. Red Cross, Girl Scouts, she collected for everything, being therefore a kind of moral neighborhood scourge. "It's a thankless job, people see you coming, they finally hate you," she would go on, but obviously secretly relishing the role. A sad stringbean of a woman, she lived a widow's pensioned existence of which this was one way of getting her out of the house, on rounds of mercy that at the same time slaked an inner spite of those more fortunate. Because there was nothing charitable about the way she used charities to blackmail you, and blackmail is good because she freely blabbed about how much everyone gave, which probably kept her quotas topping those of any block captain in all of Cook County. "Gives two dollars, and him vice-president of such and such," or "I even got one fifty-cent piece last night, imagine, and guess from who. That one getting into her Oldsmobile over there. Wouldn't you know?" These figures were openly aired at the klatsches across the street, of which she was, as I say, an uneasy member and knew it. She sensed she didn't fit, scarcely anywhere, one of those poor souls who simply give off the wrong vibes and nothing to be done about it, world without end. I scribbled off a check for five bucks for whatever cause it was, knowing there'd be another in a month, maybe less. Little did I dream how much sooner than that I'd lay eyes on Mrs. Bowser, or under what circumstances.

I made a pass at looking for part-time work, not knowing myself whether I meant it or not. I answered a few Help Wanted ads, and left the paper lying around open to the classified section, with a few of the entries circled in pencil. I saw Mrs. Landgrabber regularly, once a week at least, more when her husband was out of town and the confidence he wouldn't turn up unexpectedly was absolute. We made love on a couch in the rumpus room downstairs, her aversion to "violating the marriage bed" being quite sincere, as it was with me, something we both took quite literally. I feel there are moral laws that should be followed to the letter, not given mere lip service, though I know that is not a fashionable viewpoint in your sophisticated world of today. I was rather shocked to see the hero in a well thought of Broadway comedy take his playmate into his own and his wife's bedroom. We would lie together, Rochelle and I, in the "dim religious light" cast just exactly right through the half-open door of the rumpus room from a lamp burning on a hallway stair. Afterward we would roam around the house in the raw, foraging for snacks or just rapping. Sometimes I'd amuse her by putting on her stockings, or wearing her underpants for a hat. Man *is* a natural homebody, no use in denying it. The sciences have got to recognize it. Yes, domesticity *is* an instinct, just as well as sex. How cozy this was, a haven from the spiritual bankruptcy and moral squalor of the times.

One day in the course of one of those rambling post-love bull sessions that are such a happy part of the sexual relation I stepped into the parlor to fish a cigarette out of a box on the table there. It stood next to a window through which the front porch of the house was visible, and vice versa. As I raised the lid of the box the doorbell rang, and Mrs. Bowser and I stood facing each other through the leaded pane of bungalow glass, she in one of the faded cloth coats that had become the very armor and battle-dress of her dreary, nagging, relentless pursuit, I in the buff except for trunks and a completely unbuttoned shirt. I dropped the box like a hot potato and shot out of sight, thereby cancelling out whatever doubts might have remained about my presence there and then.

Mrs. Landgrabber was fortunately in a dress and slippers and could answer the door, as after a brief demented whispered consultation we decided she'd better do, but what good was that? I stood in the kitchen beating my fists against the sides of my head as I listened to the brief transaction at the door and then the door close. When Mrs. Landgrabber walked back there with the bag out of which she had dug the currency contributed I was still at it. "Sonofa*bitch*. Why did I run? That was it. I should have acted natural, even gone to the door with you, said I was helping you paper a room, hence the garb, *anything*." It was another rotten break from one of those unrecallable reflexes of which I seemed to be the victim.

Mrs. Landgrabber was standing there still holding the bag by the strap, the bag open, her mouth hanging open too in slack-jawed idiocy.

"Al. You mean she saw you? Like that? Al?"

"She saw me. We were that far apart. Christ, don't stand there agreeing with me it's that bad. Say something qualifying, the bright side. A ray of hope, please."

"There isn't any bright side." Her voice was toneless, the bag dangling from her leaden arm the way her arm dangled from its shoulder. "There isn't any ray of hope. She's a notorious gossip. George says she's the opposite of those three oriental monkeys. See all evil, hear all evil, speak all evil. She's those three monkeys in reverse and all rolled into one. George says."

"Don't stand there quoting George for once. He doesn't have anything to do with this."

"He will." A zombie, she stared straight ahead, at nothing. She was as dead. "What do you weight in as? What would you say you are? Welterweight, light heavyweight . . . ?"

"How much did you give her?"

"A dollar eighty-five."

"A dollar eighty-*five*? Who gives amounts like that? It's like the price of something in a department store, for God's sake. People give in round numbers."

"It was all I had."

"What's it for?"

"Little League."

I sat down at the table and beat my head against it. She watched me, her interest seemingly revived by it. "You can do that later," she said. "We've got to get our wits about us and try to think of a story. Something that'll hold water, as an explanation of why you were here. Something we can tell both George and your wife before it gets to their ears from other sources."

Over some strong black coffee I racked my brains, carrying the cup as I paced the floor. I finally came up with something, probably the result of a train of associations with her remark that it should hold water.

"How's this? Your cellar was flooded. A pipe burst, flooding the cellar. The water rose ever higher, in panic you telephoned me, I dashed right over, stripped to my shorts and waded in there to bail that water out. I kept this up till the plumber arrived."

I consulted Mrs. Landgrabber's face as a gauge of the intelligence of this suggestion. She nodded, then shook her head. "Yes and no. It's all right to tell your wife, who'd have no reason to doubt the story, or to check up on it. What your day was like and so on. But George would know from one look at the basement it wasn't true. He's due in tonight from Frisco. Everything will be in order down there. He'll see there's no busted pipe."

"I'll *bust* one." I prowled the floor, setting the cup down and smacking a fist into a palm. "I'll bust a pipe myself. I'll flood the damn basement in person, so we won't *have* to make up the story. It'll be true."

She shook her head. "It's no good. There's a drain down there any water from busted pipes would run right down. No bailing out would be necessary. That's only in cartoons, those flooded basements. Where people are wading to their waist in water. You're a romantic."

"I'll plug the goddam *drain*. I'll plug up the drain *then* bust the goddam pipe. Get me a bag of sand, where's a sledgehammer?"

"You'd better go home. The only busting that will be done around here if the story gets out will be by George. And I guess you know what he'll bust. You'd better go on home. Go home to your wife. She'll be home from work soon, the same as my husband. Oh, why was I born. This is no life."

"You have your art."

"That's only a vicarious substitute."

"What kind of a substitute?"

"Go. Put your clothes on and go. Please."

I ran into the nemesis only a day or two later, sloping toward me down the street, huddled into another thin coat and clutching her block captain's kit. I checked another reflex to dart across to the other side, instead installing a smile on my face as I strode up to meet her.

"Afternoon, Miz Bowser. Was that you at the Land-grabbers' the other day? Because I didn't know which end was up at that point. She'd called to say her basement was flooded and I worked like a demon bailing it out. Thank God the plumber came right after you left. I was up to my waist in water."

The thin nose bent to the right, inhaling a sniff of air. "I hope it wasn't hot water."

"No, nothing like that." What was this, a drawing room comedy? I didn't pause to dwell on her gift of repartee, because I noticed something that confirmed a suspicion developed during the klatsches. You have probably met up with people who have a habit, or compulsion or whatever it is, of repeating what they have just said, under their breath? A queer quirk. Now with horror I saw her look away across the street and whisper, "I hope it wasn't hot water." I was mixed up with a madwoman, or at least a dangerous neurotic, as I detained her long enough to find out.

"How are you coming along with — what is it now, Little League? A very worthy cause, as the contributions I regularly make show I feel."

"Not as well as it might, if they'd stick to the spring for their drive. There are so many in the fall. People are more baseball-minded in the spring. I don't know what possessed them to switch." Then as the chills ran up my spine she repeated *sotto voce*, "I don't know what possessed them to switch."

"That was a very interesting discussion we had the other day I thought. On the fence. About the new freedom? How moral standards change without really damaging *the principle of human virtue itself*." Stupe! How much rope do you want to give yourself? You're only making it worse. But worse I made it. "It struck me as an especially interesting point someone made about there being no sexual morality in itself — conduct in that area should be judged in terms of the whole man. One's decency and integrity and what not, *in general*."

"I believe it was you who made that point," Mrs. Bowser said, with a smile.

"Oh, was it? I don't remember. Somebody anyway. It struck me as quite cogent at the time, in any case." It was like trying to dig myself out of a hole. "The nub of the whole thing is that right and wrong are relative matters."

"But there's still a right and wrong." She gazed off across the rooftops. "There's still a right and wrong."

"I couldn't agree with you more. I couldn't agree with you more."

"Do you know Mr. Landgrabber very well?" I began an inconclusive shrug. Then, again a faint smile on that unpreferred face, she said, "He travels a lot, doesn't he? Do you happen to know what firm he works for?"

"I believe it's the Bundy Products."

"Oh, yes. Those detergents and things. Well, goodbye, Mr. Banghart."

An ounce of prevention having the value we know, what must not a pound of it be worth. I began this prophylaxis by never slipping across to Mrs. Landgrabber's again, in whose house I saw myself in a hundred cautionary visions: classically upended in a closet, the door of which the homecoming husband rips open to find nothing — but hold it, aren't those a pair of feet under the dangling suits and dresses?; shot to death in bed, perforated while in the very throes; the tar kicked out of me preparatory to being hacked to ribbons with the kitchen cleaver, the parts strewn across the blood-stained floor; told to lay off. This last the worst of all, being in the form of a telephone call received in the presence of one's wife, even *by* one's wife. "Take a message will you, for your husband? Just tell him to keep away from my wife. Never mind who this is. *He'll* know." So the pound of prevention included remarking to my wife that I'd heard there was a crackpot in the neighborhood who made accusing telephone calls, not specifying sex, since if we got one it could be either Mrs. Bowser or Mr. Landgrabber. So I left that open.

The blow fell in quite another way, though obviously set in motion by a call, or anonymous letter, from the one to the other, at his office now that she knew where it was.

It was late afternoon in November. I was in the kitchen getting my roast on. I thought a leg of lamb seen at the market would be nice, with some nice potatoes, and maybe a few nice carrots. (Why do women call all these things nice even before they've bought them?) It was the tag-end of Indian summer. I had the windows open, as did the Landgrabbers, judging from a high-fidelity reception I was getting from a quarrel raging there. Or not quarrel as much as a prolonged unilateral blast from Himself, the words of which floated in to me on the balmy air. He had obviously heard. The names he called Rochelle were such that "two-timing Jezebel" was one of the milder, and his tone rose steadily to a pitch suggesting that one version or another of the above-described mayheims was about to begin with her the object — and me next. Because he rumbled away on the basis of that being the agenda. "And when I finish with you, I'll go next door and hand him his head."

I stood frozen by the window. Should I beat it? Should I stay and brazen it out? Better a live dog than a dead lion, the prophet said. Should I seize the initiative by phoning the Landgrabbers and innocently asking, "By the way, have you by any chance had any anonymous phone calls from that crackpot who seems to be spreading imaginary scandals about people? Because I just had another, and we were wondering . . ." More prophylaxis, possibly too late, maybe not. But I didn't. I stood there in a kind of paralytic awe listening to a *tirade* as it should really be delivered. Still he didn't come and he didn't come. I heard the loud clink of bottle and glass, meaning he was probably fueling up. I could use a little Dutch courage myself, and poured myself some. Gulping it down, I thought: "Or you can hide in your own closet. That'd be a switch. I don't think it's ever been done, even in a television sketch." Of course the feet visible under the dangling garments would probably be mandatory . . .

While creative energies were thus dissipated in vain story-line fancies, the vulgar scene next door bowled on toward its climax. I frantically reviewed the telephone-call device one more time, finally deciding that my mention of a whispering campaign to my wife was safe-guard enough. After all it was only her opinion I was interested in, assuming I survived whatever fate George had in store for me. I glanced nervously at the clock. A quarter to five. More than time for Rose to be getting home, though she had said something about a teachers' meeting. I had wandered to the front of the house with my drink, for a look out the window, and now went back to the kitchen. We had spoken of catching a movie, so an early dinner was important. I put my roast in the oven, hearing nothing more next door. Had Landgrabber talked himself out? The silence continued for some minutes. Then I heard both voices, lowered. Mrs. Landgrabber was saying, "— talk it over like two civilized people." Or maybe it was four! I couldn't catch it all, but my God, what if George took that insane idea into his head. I was almost relieved to hear his diatribe resumed. It culminated in his thundering out the back door, down the stairs and toward the alley gate. Rooted where I stood, I heard my own gate squeak open and then his footsteps marching up the walk to the porch. There was a banging on the door.

"Come in."

Landgrabber was clearly three sheets. His blue eyes were at once bleary and glittering, and his bald head exaggerated the blaze of anger in which he entered, being as red as his face. He had thick sideburns running nearly down to his jaw, one longer than the other, which added to the general dishevelment also contributed to by a loose collar and tie.

"Mmyes?"

I had my roast in the oven and was getting my potatoes on. I had my apron tied around my middle. The picture these details and others added up to made his jaw drop. His outburst came to a halt before it got started. He stood there and goggled at the sight. He could not believe, would not believe, that anybody like what he was gaping at could have cuckolded him. His ego would not have it. His vanity could not brook it. It was out.

"Mmwell?" I queries again, wetting a middle fingertip and smoothing an eyebrow. My instinct instantly picked up the cue telling me how to play it. I didn't even have to think. I knew salvation lay in that absolute and flabbergasted disbelief. The kitchen props and house-apron enabled me to camp it up for a fare-thee-well. "What were you saying? What theems to be the trouble, Mr. Landgrabber? Is thumthing exerthising you?"

He gulped a few times and took a step farther into the room.

"Well, it's something I heard. About you and my missus." He dropped his eyes guiltily to the floor.

"Oh, that." I waved him off with a willowy wrist as I minced toward the refrigerator for some ice cubes. "I thimply adore her, I think she's thimply a thmasher, and I wish it were true. Tee-hee." Watch it, I said to myself, not so thick. I drove in the nail I had in readiness. "Somebody call you on the phone?" I continued, easing up on the lisp. "Woman with a high raspy voice?"

He gave a dazed nod. "Yeah."

"Oh, Gawd," I said, the back of the hand held limply to the brow, eyes rolling. "Must be the same one who telephoned anonymously here and asked did I realize my wife was fooling around with somebody. A neighbor." I giggled again. "Thought it might be you. My wife keeps throwing up to me that bald men are more virile. Makes me so cross. You probably *are* full of the old

Nick," I said, sweeping him with a look and wagging one shoulder.

"Yeah . . ." He simpered, still looking at the floor. He shifted his weight from one foot to the other.

"Well, anyway, don't let it worry you. Anybody who is anybody is getting these calls, though they're beginning to bore some of us to a frazzle. Finally got around to you, eh?" My mind racing like lightning, I wondered whether I was leaving any stone unturned. Whether there was anything I had overheard that would leave any bugs in this flummery. Mrs. Landgrabber had said something about talking it over like civilized people. That could mean merely the rumor, not an admitted intrigue.

"Can I fix you a drink?" I said, confident that I had tucked in any loose ends I knew of. "I'm just freshening up this highball of mine. Won't you sit down? Come have one with me, man. I've got my dinner on."

"No . . . No, thanks. I'd better get back. I got all fired up, naturally, when I heard this. You can understand that."

"Of course. Your going berserk does you credit. Well, goodbye then, Mr. Landgrabber. Come over some time and we'll lift a few. You and the missus with me and my missus. MmmO.K.?"

"Swell. Well, so long."

At the sight of his back I dropped into a chair and collapsed in ecstatic relief. "Phew," I said aloud, and drank to my narrow squeak. A little prematurely.

I heard a footstep in the other direction from that in

which Mr. Landgrabber's chastened clomp was receding. Looking over, I saw my wife in the doorway. She still had her coat on and was still clutching her briefcase. She had come in the front door without my knowing it.

"I heard most of that," she said.

"Then I don't have to tell you. *Wild?* Remember what I said about those poison-pen phone calls people have been getting?"

"It's true. Isn't it?"

"What?"

"About you and Mrs. Landgrabber. You've been having an affair with her."

"Pshaw."

"Never mind that. It's not your kind of language, and not all that's ringing false. I knew there was something fishy about that phone-call talk. The way you kept dragging it in. I suspected something funny then. Now I know. It's true. What he accused you of, or started to before you threw him off fruiting it up like that. Pretty nifty, even without all that taradiddle about crackpot calls. His was probably legitimate."

"Oh, come now." My potatoes were boiling over and I hurried to the stove to turn the flame down, grasping the pot-handle in my apron. "Your imagination is running away with you."

"No, it's yours that's standing you in good stead. Rat."

When I could bring myself to raise my eyes, I was in for the surprise of my life. She was smiling, a smile of reproach, her head to one side, so that she looked at me askance. "You rat," she softly murmured again. Reader, she wanted it to be true. "You louse, you dog, you snake," she ran on.

I looked at the floor, my lips curling into a simper that must have been a lot like Landgrabber's own.

"I knew there must be some reason you wanted to stay home — or I mean I should have known. It gave you the perfect chance to play the lady-killer. Isn't that it? Fess up. Of course. I should have known."

"Then you're calling off the divorce?"

"Now that I know you've been unfaithful, yes. The life you were leading that I couldn't endure was only a front for that. It's a relief to me, really, more than anything else. Anything but to have to believe that there was nothing more to the potato-peeling floor-sweeping character she left behind every morning than met the eye."

I dug this, completely. It was a fine point of feminine psychology, but a firm one. Now she needn't go around apologizing for a Milquetoast. She could hold her head up, knowing what everybody else would soon know, about what she had been woman enough to bag. Something like that. I had redeemed myself in her eyes. All that came out more clearly as I questioned her about her feelings and we discussed our mutual problem openly. The nagging set of alternatives once blurted — was I a man or a mouse — was now resolved. I was neither. I was a rat. Not an ideal revelation, but a compromise, one she could live with — along with the hope that eventually that would be improved on. Because the potential was still there. I would bend every effort myself to realize it. I gave her credit for trying to build me up, in a way and to an extent I probably didn't deserve, as I saw in my heart of hearts.

But at the end of that long and soul-searching evening, just when I thought I understood all this, she made a remark that put me back completely in left field.

"Tell me something, though," I said. "Why do women go to such lengths to prop up what they really consider the weaker sex? To build a husband up the way some of them do?"

She gazed thoughtfully over my head a moment and said, "Let's just say chivalry isn't dead."

Which goes to show you the difficulty of ever understanding what the hell women are talking about, a good half the time.

6

If the number of leaves a man turns over in a lifetime
is any gauge of his sincerity there can be little doubt of
mine. I went to work selling things door-to-door, Christmas cards, magazine subscriptions, key rings with small
flashlights attached to them for use in the dark, making
my pitches with a pretended speech defect to enlist the
sympathies of prospective buyers. "Ood morning,
ma'am. I'm hjelling heese hings made by hmeeple more
unforhunate han me." Sometimes I varied this, or even
supplemented it, by hobbling along with a limp. I never
took home much money, but I took home some, besides,
of course, the satisfaction and pride in doing an honest

day's work. We were able to move out of that neighborhood into a better one, and needless to say I never saw Mrs. Landgrabber again. The shakeup had given me a moral rebirth to which the previous one couldn't be compared.

One day at the end of my rounds I ran into our minister, Shorty Hopwell, out shopping for religious supplies, such as red Burgundies august enough to be our Lord's propitiatory blood. Actually I spots him in a package store where I was window-shopping. He was standing over a display of new shipments in wicker baskets, holding a bottle in each hand, comparing them in consultation with a salesman, who was showing him a small card, probably one of those vintage charts rating the different years. I assumed the discreet little Beaujolais we'd had at recent communions was all used up. When Shorty came out, with both bottles, to try them I suppose before going into case quantities, I buttonholed him.

"Hi, Hjnorty," I said, with the last of the day's speech habits not quite shaken off, and still dragging a foot. "How about a hwick sjnort?" For eventide was now come, and he must needs sup with me and I with him, that we might abide with one another. Feeley's was just around the corner, and thither we repairs.

The lucky stroke about this wasn't in my bumping into Shorty like that but in our both running into Artie Carpenter — Tut Carpenter's brother, remember? — and hauling him into Feeley's with us. He was always glad to see me, being eternally grateful Tut hadn't married me. Or The Stopped Up Sink. His joy knew no bounds. He was going great guns in a branch of electronic research that gave him valuable ties with recording outfits. Hearing I wasn't happy as a field representative for an ever-changing line of products, he offered to speak to a friend of his who was high up among the executives of a newly formed corporation called Peerless Records. That was how I got a proper nine-to-five job.

I liked it in the outer office at Peerless. Besides me there were two women there. Miss Tompkins was a maiden lady in her forties, Miss Balfour a plump, dewey creature half that age. I naturally lost no time in seeing whether we were programmed for each other. I took her to lunch a few times in the only restaurant near there, a hole-in-the-wall delicatessen where the food arrived with a speed she said was "vulgar," however explainable as the management's need and desire to get you off those tables so they could feed your successors, who were standing over you slavering impatiently and giving you nasty glares if you tried to dawdle over your coffee in what Miss Balfour called "some semblance of civilized leisure in this world of crass haste." She knew all that stuff. Once I had the distinct impression that strings of saliva were definitely hanging from one such waiting beast, although the wolf leer on his face, complete with gleaming fangs, suggested the secretions may at least in part have been the result of the advantageous view he had of Miss Balfour's cleavage and attendant dumplings, which had my own juices flowing as well.

But it was not what you'd call refined and gracious living. The powers that be'd were not exactly grooming me for administrative roles, that I knew, and so I was hardly surprised to have them call me into the adjacent stockroom now and then for a little pushing and shoving, to say nothing of putting the over-stimulated salivary glands to work on a spot of label-sticking. Rolling a shirtsleeve down one day after a stint in the stockroom, preparatory to putting my coat back on in the outer office, I had to cope again with a button missing from the cuff. I finally fastened it with a stapling machine I had on my desk. Miss Balfour took this in with a melting gaze.

"You need someone to look after you," she said.

I muttered something about not believing a woman's job was to be a domestic slave.

"But the one you marry will at least have to send you out into the world in one piece. Stapling a cuff!"

"That's right," I laughed.

A few minutes later, when we were all working at our desks again, a sudden downpour began.

"Coming down in buckets," she mused. "Kind of weather you like to lie in bed listening to. For *hours*. I can be insanely lazy."

Miss Tompkins cleared her throat with an expression saying she personally lacked that characteristic, and that it was not high on her list of regrets. When Miss Balfour continued to dilate on the rain, I finally said, "Oh, by the way, would you look out and see if it's falling on the just and the unjust, there's a dear."

The roselips parted in a blank stare. "See . . . ?" She transferred the baby blues from me to the window, for a gander into the street. Miss Tompkins gave me a conspiring smile, as though to say it was her and me who were the kindred spirits around here, the intellectual companions. "Well, they're all scurrying for cover, that's for sure," Miss Balfour reported. "Has the sound of those rains that settle in for a good long while too. I don't know how I'll ever get home."

I was disturbed to find myself speculating on how nice it would be to take her there. This moral reclamation stuff is like painting the Brooklyn Bridge — perpetual. You no more than get to one end than you have to go back and start all over again from the beginning. It's very discouraging. I was as relieved as I was sorry to see her quit, as she did shortly afterward, leaving only Miss Tompkins to take to the only restaurant in the neighborhood, since they showed no signs of replacing Miss Balfour. I shouldn't be that hard on Miss Tompkins, with whom I found I could rap as you can with a woman with whom all bets are off, sexually. (Rose's explanation of why women can rap so well with fags, like at parties.) She was handsomely built, though lacking in that final element that makes or breaks a woman's figure — a good walk. Hips alone mean nothing, they've got to roll right. Any man knows he can't grade a woman in that department until he's seen her strolling, and away from him. Then she either has that extra gelatin or she doesn't. Miss Tompkins' tail was like a summer cold. She couldn't seem to shake it. But it was a sandwich with her in the deli, underneath the over-hanging humanoids, that produced the next stage in my progress. It was from her I learned what I hadn't known, that Peerless had a few openings for salesmen. I went straight to the front office and got them to give me a chance to show what I could do. I said I'd had some experience selling for a recording outfit I happened to know was defunct, so they couldn't check. The man I talked to, Allbright, seemed to think my being a singer myself, though only of sorts and however erstwhile, would deepen my grasp of at least the popular enter-tainers whose platters I would now be peddling from store to store — hardly the same thing as from door to door — and I chattered knowledgeably about "the charts" I had been boning up on in recent issues of *Variety*. I went to work on a tryout basis two weeks later, armed with Peerless's new spring catalogue.

With both of us working and most of our dinners eaten out, good restaurants became important, the more so when, to get a foothold, I began wining and dining some of my clients. That was Rose's idea. "What if you do use up all your salary at first? We can live on mine," she said. "But for God's sake let's get out of Feeley's. Get Feeley's out of your system."

"I thought it was our place."

"I thought the El Conquistador was. Maybe it's too early to tell. But the last time you took me to dinner at Feeley's there was a piece of shrapnel in my ground chuck steak. I like atmosphere too, but not that much."

She was wearing a blue-and-white striped suit with matching eyeshadow, so what could I say?

Thus it was that restaurants became a sort of theme of that chapter of my life. It can be told almost entirely in terms of them. I hated to repudiate Feeley, who had symbolized my single days. I realized he was part of the origins I must rise above, but still. Many's the word of advice he had dished out to me in classic bartender style, good advice too, though liberally interlarded with "duhs." "She's got style, class, all around — duh — refinement," he had said from the start about Rose, the fifth column. "Snap her up. You get her you're getting a lady with — duh — criterions." This was counsel I couldn't take without renouncing the giver and his joint, and I did so with regret. All the more so because Feeley's parting word of wisdom was intended to help launch me on a career that was partly the reason for my ditching him. Drawing on his own early years as a salesman, he said, "Want a tip, Al? The best way to warm up a prospect is get him on some subject having nothing to do with the product. Like his hobby. Or even better yet I found, his habits." Here he leaned closer toward me over the bar, continuing with that, now, acumen imputed to tavern-keepers everywhere. "Ever notice how solemn we all get when we talk about our habits? As though they're sacred, which they are — to us. They *are* us. Well, my boy, get a buyer talking about what he eats for breakfast, when he goes to bed, his bathing routines, anything, even the order he puts his shoes on. It gets him into an, I don't know, comfortable mood.

Hard to explain exactly why. Psychologists say our habits are a sort of private — duh — ritual. No wonder they're sacred, for cry bones," Feeley finished, with one of those slang terms that seemed to me peculiar, not just to Chicago, but only certain sections of that. I've never heard it anywhere else.

This is advice valuable for warming up others than business prospects. Such as guests. If you spot one in your house who's bored, get him on the subject of his habits and see how quickly he springs to life. The merest remark or question will nudge a given pooper around to it. Of course he may *become* a bore, but he'll no longer *be* bored, and thus spread that contagion through the party. Anyway, that was one of the major pieces of advice my Polonius sped me off into the world with.

Among my most important clients, and the first of my deductible dinner guests, were the Boxfords. They ran the biggest phonograph and record store in my South Side territory (where I had ordered the Burton-Donne reading). I had never seen the place as crowded as it was the day I made my first call there, armed with my Peerless catalogue. I waited over an hour for the chance to show it to them. Mrs. Boxford shrugged her fat shoulders apologetically from the cluster of customers that never seemed to thin out, glancing toward her husband who was just as occupied selling phonograph and TV sets as she was in the platter section. It was then I laughed and suggested they might like to talk over dinner, a proposal on which she pounced. Rose wanted to try a well-known French restaurant just off Hyde Park Boulevard, and it was for this we headed in my new Chevrolet, the oversized Boxfords winding up some argument or other as they settled down in the back seat. I could see them in the rearview mirror, a good quarter-ton of public domesticity. "He keeps thinking we're running a discount store, that's the misconception he keeps laboring under," Mrs. Boxford said, pointing a thumb at her husband, who grinned as he raked hair as thick and yellow naturally as hers was pharmaceutically. "Especially when some Twin Peaks comes in there and makes googoos at him. Eh, Boxford? Then we knock off ten percent *at least.*"

"Very funny," he kept repeating, at thrusts that never seemed to be meant as such. It put their controversy in a peculiar fuzzy focus, as though you were hearing double the way you sometimes see double. I hurried to the restaurant so I could begin to quiz them about their habits over a drink or two.

We got a good table near the bandstand, if that's a good table, for there was dancing there, and some prompt service from a burly blond with huge horn-rimmed glasses through which he openly appreciated the ladies, especially Mrs. Boxford's expanse of bare shoulders. "You pen to de peach, rushing de season, ja? Or south mit de sun to Florida maybe? I can tell by de freggles dot you oggwired," said the waiter in this well-known French restaurant. It wasn't until we'd had a few drinks and were attacking our appetizers that I spotted an opening for my sales technique.

"I noticed you put salt on your canteloupe," I said to Boxford. "That's very interesting."

He nodded soberly. "Yes, there are some of us who do that. And you know what else we do?" I saw that he wagged his spoon when he talked, but that wasn't what he meant. He lowered his voice, as though the practice he was about to divulge was some kind of perversion, or at least colorful specialty. I was all ears. "Those of us who put salt on melons — watermelon, anything — most of us who do that will also go to work and put sugar on tomatoes. Fact."

"Well, I'll be damned," I said. "That's most interesting. Did you hear that, dear? Mr. Boxford puts salt on melons and sugar on tomatoes. Just the other way around from the general public."

"From the common herd," Rose nodded. She was clearly enjoying herself, oblivious to the danger I now began to sense from another quarter.

Mrs. Boxford hadn't said anything for some time, but you could tell she was tuning up, either to resume the argument she'd been having with Boxford or to vent her feelings in another one. She snuffled ominously as she hunched over the remains of her third whiskey sour, clearing her throat as though about to let loose with some of the ammunition she'd been collecting in her mind, God knew how long. Maybe fifty years. There are certain women who seem to need public displays of their private feelings — public tears, public fights. It's their particular form of, now, catharsis. Yes, this dilly was plainly revving up her motors.

"Us more ordinary mortals," I said with a sociable laugh in Boxford's direction, "can understand sugar on tomatoes, but salt on melons . . ." I shook my head at the amazing uniqueness of this. Mrs. Boxford jerked erect.

"He likes other kinds of tomatoes than those you grow in gardens."

"Weeell," I says, spreading my hands with a general look around. "Don't we all."

"Which is why we can only hire male help."

"For her," says Boxford, waving his head at his wife without looking at her. He was smiling, but I noticed his nostrils tauten, and his pink skin began to mottle, till it resembled his wife's freckled shoulders.

"That's not true."

"It is."

"So contradicting me is another of his habits, as you can see."

"They can also see where I picked it up. Out of necessity. Or call it self-defense. Because I think you'll find it largely true that husbands don't punch — they only counterpunch."

"Tell me," I says, "will you go to work and put salt on other melons too? I mean besides a muskmelon?"

"Christ, I just told you that. *All melons.*"

"Ah, yes. Of course."

Rose chimed in here, clapping her hands. "I haven't

heard that word for years — muskmelon. I'd forgotten people used to call them that. I think it's a wonderful word, don't you? So much more expressive than canteloupe."

"But better for honeydews than for canteloupe," I said. "They have more of a smell. So that would include honeydews too, Mr. Boxford? Your 'all melons'? You go for honeydews, fellow?"

"Oh, definitely," says the wife. "Especially if they're in a brassiere." She gave a sharp amused cackle.

"What's the matter with topless?" came from Boxford.

I laughed at this, as you do at the client's jokes, rule number one any drummer knows. But it had an absolutely unavoidable backlash. The wife took herself to be the butt both of the brainless comeback and the artificially extruded yack, and the hostile undercurrent became a boiling stream, sweeping us all toward the falls in our helplessly twirling little skiff.

"A lot of good it would do him if it was," says sweetie pie, and sits back as though she's delivered the knockout punch. But I seemed to have lost the thread and so didn't know exactly where the wit in this resided. Therefore to give her the benefit of the doubt, and another possible boff from me, I asked, "A lot of good what would do who if what was?"

"Him, if it was topless! Or even bottomless! He's not going anywhere. He's been."

"Oh yeah?" snaps the other combatant. "As your ban on female help in the shop would indicate?"

"It's just that the turnover isn't so high if we hire men. Not so many walking out on the famous melon squeezer. Pinchers don't always buy."

"Oh yeah?" Boxford was merely stalling till he could think of a retort. You could sense his own mental wheels turning while he played for time. The delay was like a clinch in which two equally matched prizefighters momentarily lock themselves to catch their breath. Lady Bountiful elegantly pried a fragment of food from between her lower teeth with a thumbnail and retorted: "Yeah. You'd think we were running a fruit store."

That was leading with her chin, as she instantly realized. We all saw the opening, and the glove swinging inevitably into it.

"Maybe we are, the kind of guys you hire," said Boxford. "Maybe you go for that type. *They themselves* are famous for preferring women —"

"Shall we dance?"

This from my smiling Rose, who had for some time been softly then ever more loudly rapping a spoon on the edge of the table in rhythm with the orchestra that had struck up. Her question was directed to Boxford, who rose with a courtly bow, livid with rage. Mrs. Boxford and I watched them till they reached the dance floor, then turned back to each other with the stuffed-lynx grins that were now the order of the evening. Miss Piano once told us in class that there was a theory of humor, propounded by some philosopher whose name I don't recall but endorsed by Aldous Huxley, that analyzed laughter as a "civilized snarl," a human version of the baring of the teeth that accompanies animal aggression. The hypothesis certainly fit this night's little jollification. Alone with the captive audience she really wanted, Mrs. Boxford now took up that sub-category of gripes a not-so-quietly desperate woman might be expected to find her ultimate satisfaction in ventilating. Her husband's sexual habits. I did my best not to hear what she was saying, clearing my throat or shifting my chair or calling the waiter to censor out key words you could anticipate coming up, grateful also for the growing din of the orchestra and the dancers on the floor.

"There are men who need certain kicks, often of the kind that subjugates the woman," she said. "Well, before Boxford can achieve —"

"Ah, my favorite waltz I believe. May I have this one?"

I half carried her not only to the floor but around it, she was by now that sodden. Once or twice we passed the other pair. Rose was beaming with that pretended oblivion to horror for which she had a knack, though maybe it was the grace of someone secure in her superiority to the Neanderthals putting us through this. Maybe she secretly *enjoyed* it. I don't know. Not even married people have access to one another's final interiors, probably a damn good thing in the long run. But I wanted to swat and pin a medal on her both. Boxford was piloting her grimly around the floor, his face now a dangerous shade of lavender, drawing deep breaths that sucked in his nostrils, so that the end of his nose looked as though it was clamped together with an invisible clothespin. I didn't like the looks of this. I was even afraid we might be getting into Cardiac Country. And all because I had opened my trap to inquire about a lousy canteloupe! Why weren't we sitting around telling stories like the one about the maiden who set a musk-melon in the window as a sign to her lover that they couldn't run away that night? (Can't elope.)

"Habits? I'll tell you about habits."

"I don't think you should talk like this."

That was a mistake. It had only the effect of pulling out another stop, because now she had to justify herself, and the surest way to do that was to certify her griev-ance by showing me I hadn't heard anything yet. The ensuing cannibalism bit was one Boxford probably had a hunch she was on, judging by the looks he kept shoot-ing in our direction. I steered my Scheherazade as often as I could into his general neighborhood, saying some-thing like "Yes, we certainly have had an early spring," or "Oh, you really feel that about this administration?" as we staggered on by. But the glare of that eyeball grew more terrible, arguing badly for anything in the way of fat orders. I beat my partner back to the table by a good ten paces, just to keep her out of earshot. The others returned about then, as did the waiter with the trout amandine we had all ordered.

"Well!" I said, falling to. "Has anybody else read that report about fish contamination in the Hudson River? They estimate we've got about thirty-five years left on this planet." So we talked about something pleasant for a change. Plus which I drank till I didn't really give a damn what I heard any more, the old liquid lobotomy that sees us through many an ordeal by temporarily cutting off the higher brain centers. The culprit and the cure are identical, as you've no doubt found at disaster parties. The same booze that lets the worms out of some poor bastard's woodwork enables you to sit there and smile at the sight of them crawling across the hostess's carpet and even up your leg. I had long since written this little old nocturne off by the time Boxford got around to glaring at me and muttering, "Get a woman to badmouth her husband by talking about his habits. Some people will do anything for hacks. Guess we know where to take our business now . . ." "Yeah," Mrs. Boxford mumbled, now joining forces with him in some shift of emotion I didn't even try to fathom. I had to say to myself what I'd wanted to say to each of them all evening: "How about a little infinite understanding?"

"Well, that was nice," I says to Rose when we had dropped our waterlogged and by now probably amorous cargo.

"You were superb."

What followed was something I had been steeling myself for, and thanked God didn't happen till after we'd gotten rid of the Boxfords.

On the "perb" of "superb," Rose's voice tailed upward in that little squeal well known to me as signalling another fit of hysterics. She was still helplessly convulsed an hour later, when we were in bed, she on her side, turned away from me, I propped up moodily sucking a cigar as befitted my new station in life. The spring jiggled steadily under us, like those motel beds that massage you by vibration when you put a quarter in the meter. She couldn't stop till she had run her course, like those mechanisms themselves. And I didn't expect her to. After all, it was one of her more familar habits.

These were only two of the many people with whom we ate out in that period of my life of which, as I say, restaurants were the keynote. Most of them were friends rather than clients or business associates, and not all of the latter were as hairy as the Boxfords (who turned out to be a poor test of Feeley's advice, which I found generally sound). Some were office connections turned friends. But our rise in the world was told in our public dining. I say "our" because one night we went out to celebrate Rose's sale of an article, "Teaching a Language by Teaching Its Literature," to a national magazine. We thought we'd try another French restaurant, Hercule's. Rose shimmered in a new blue dress of shot silk.

"I wonder how the cuisine is here," she said, opening her menu.

"Excellent. They fix it with a white wine sauce."

"Come now, Al, you're not at Feeley's now." It was mock pedagogy, but at the same time she glanced worriedly at the captain to see if he was in earshot, in a way that told me, "No more goon stuff." She closed the menu and put it by with a "You order for both of us." Thus compelling me with a pretty flourish to play the debonair host. She had many such tactful little wiles, for helping me rise above my origins.

So Excelsior! Ever upward! The menus began to have tassels on them, the wine lists with their watered silk and vellum bindings to resemble diplomas I was being handed for graduating from something — which in a sense I was. And the food! What will you have first, my dear? O slices of golden Cranshaw like quarter-moons! O clams casino! O bowls of cracked crab, of gazpacho, of lobster bisque! And the ambiance I think they call it! Who are those at nearby tables? There's So-and-so the noted co-producer. There's What's-his-name, author of over a dozen promising novels. And isn't that the British actress who recently locked her husband out of their apartment, in bitter winter weather? The absolute *crème de la crème*. The beautiful people all.

Six months after becoming a salesman for Peerless Records I was kicked upstairs. They tried me on writing catalogue and envelope copy for popular releases, and it worked out. To celebrate the promotion one of the vice-presidents took us out, with his wife, a chick as slick as a peeled scallion. Our Al now finds himself in a restaurant that makes his head swim. It is called The Palms, apparently not only for those fluttering in pots beside a plashing fountain, but also those that must be greased in order not to wind up behind said foliage, peering enviously at those with decent tables, like monkeys in a Rousseau painting. The menus here were the size of pup tents. The four of us stayed totally eclipsed from one another for fifteen minutes, while we studied the things that we were torn between. Mrs. Pomeroy, the veep's wife, is so torn between the shrimps Arnaud and the cheddar cheese soup that she has to let her husband decide, and that's only the beginning. Graver crises are posed by sweetbreads Gramercy and breast of capon and orange duck, and there is no use even in going into the cruel dilemmas the desserts impale you on. Our Al Banghart sees that he has indeed arrived. No more, "Oh, I see they've got soup du jour today. I love that." Uh-uh. No more of that goon stuff. That all lies far, far behind him, part of another life so remote, so alien, it must be that of another person. The identity crisis is over. He Knows Who He Is.

The feast lies heavy within him for hours, though, and he finds it necessary to take a digestive mint, an advertised little stomachic capable of absorbing forty-seven times its weight in excess acidity. The thought of this chemical engagement going on inside you is hardly a sedative one. Is he developing ulcers? Could be. The pressure of his responsibilities intensifies, as do the marital tensions that grow as Al's share of the rat race becomes matched by his wife's on the social end of their upward climb. They have now been married four years, and are of course living in a better neighborhood still. They have a five-room studio apartment on the Gold Coast. Rose has a job teaching in a high-grade private school nearby. They are miles from their South Side origins.

"Christ, are we going out again?"

Al sits on a bedroom *fauteuil* watching his wife try on a headpiece that looks like a nun's wimple, only mink.

"You know we're seeing the Spittlefields. We'll probably go to the —" and she names a restaurant known only heretofore in hearsay. It tops everything so far, just like all the rest. Everything is under glass, everything is flown in. The lobsters from Maine, the breadsticks from Italy, the celery from Kalamazoo. The chairs and tables have been flown in from Scandinavia. The *people* are flown in. From where else with such winter tans could they have only yesterday arrived but the Caribbean, or the Coast, or at least Florida? These diners have themselves been buttered and basted under southern skies.

"*Sacrebleu,*" says our Al that night, groaning as he kicks off his patent-leather shoes and nudges them under a dresser where he prays they will disappear from the knowledge of men. "I hope that does it for a while."

Rose consults her appointment book as she unscrews a pair of fire opal earrings I gave her for Christmas.

"We've only got the Tremaynes on Saturday night. Now look, Al." She faces me gravely, standing over the lounge on which I recline, belching acidly as I unhook the waist of my trousers. She emphasizes this as another crucial turn in our upward spiral by tapping a hairbrush in her palm. "You remember we met them at that party at the Haleys' last month?" I nod with sleepy eyes, discharging another small dyspeptic bolt against my fingertips. "He's head of Blue Label Recordings, or anyway the Chicago office. If you're ever to go any higher up the ladder, I mean in your field of general promotion, it'll probably have to be in a bigger firm, like his. Peerless has been good to you, but you yourself know they're a little shaky financially besides being a relatively small outfit, and a move to Blue Label would be marvelous. I got on fine with his wife but I don't think you had a chance to spend much time with Tremayne. He obviously likes to do the talking, so apart from making an intelligent impression, let your speech be Yea, yea, and Nay, nay."

She need not have worried. We didn't dine until after attending a play for which Tremayne had got some tickets at the last minute from a friend. If the Tremaynes could still call him that after the first act. The second act passed without incident, like its predecessor, and as the houselights went up and the audience rose for the next intermission Tremayne said, "Shall we go? I for one can do without any more of this." A proposal to which all were agreeable except me, who was getting some much-needed shuteye.

I dozed in the cab all the way to the restaurant to which we were being taken, grateful for the steady flow of chatter by the women under cover of which I could do so undetected, and that Tremayne was sitting up front with the driver and making few comments of the sort to which I must respond in a manner certifying me a ball of fire. I also thanked God for the traffic delays that stretched this ride to what would, again, top anything so far seen; something that would be where it was at, if the Tremaynes were taking you there. That you knew.

The cab swept to a stop at the curb, as Rose jabbed me in the ribs. "This looks wonderful," I heard her say.

We piled out of the back seat as Tremayne settled up with the driver. I had learned it was futile, even unwise, to try to get any part of the expense of an evening of which this suave character was host. I was still somnambulating anyway as I crossed the sidewalk and entered the place, propped up by my wife, who seemed to be trying to revive me with further right hooks to the briskets. Tremayne, looking blonder and slimmer and creamier by the minute, held a curtained door open for us. Shuffling through this portal I snapped my drooping eyelids up with an effort the better to take in the establishment about which the others were exclaiming. Even with the baby blues wide open I was a moment getting my bearings. I was probably the most dazed of all.

I saw gabardine suits and low-backed silk dresses encircling a heavy mahogany bar behind which a man in a striped shirt with sleeve-garters was dispensing drinks with a harried air. I shook my head to clear it of a hallucination to which it seemed prey. Feeley looked ten years older, rather than the three or four since I had last seen him. This was owing partly to the abundant white of the sideburns and mustaches which he had let grow out to the size of a small cotton crop, they being now again back in vogue. Everything else was the same: the red-and-white-checked café curtains hanging from their tarnished brass loops; the familiar fly-specked plate-glass window just beyond, with the owner's name in reverse in gilt circus-type letters; the fat nude smiling down from within her sooty frame over the big bar mirror. Even the nickelodeon kept its ancient corner, with half its organs missing. There was even Feeley's old brother-in-law, still favoring his bunions as he trotted among the tables in his striped bottle-washer's apron, like a sheep with the footrot, setting the flatware down in clumps.

"It's completely unspoiled," said Tremayne. "Come along, I've reserved the corner table, the one there next the pianola."

"Wonderful," Rose said. "How on earth did you ever find it?" As we followed meekly in his wake, scuffing the sawdust, she gripped my arm and whispered, "If you so much as breathe one word you know the proprietor, I'm leaving you."

"Promise?" I begins my goon smile, my jaw going moron-slack as I humorously sniffs the air. "What's that smell? Atmosphere? This place sure has milieu."

I can't wait to excuse myself once we're settled, doing so at the first opportunity by pleading a glimpse of an important client at the bar to whom it's essential at least to say hello. "Of course," says Tremayne, digging the interior with the ladies. I wedge myself in among the element roosting around the wood, and finally manage to catch Feeley's eye.

He was a moment in placing me. I must have aged too! Then his face broke into a smile without losing its chronic frown.

"Well, what you don't meet when you haven't got a gun," he said. He wiped his hand on his apron and extended it. "Long time no see. Where the hell have you been? I thought you might of gave me up for Lent."

I began an account of my activities since last seen, making apologies and excuses about moving that sounded hypocritical even to me. But Feeley wasn't really listening. He broke in with something else on his mind.

"What the hell is this all about?" he said. "I get a buck and a half for drinks that once cost six bits, and six bucks for those old two-fifty steaks you used to eat. The old-timers that still make it here — Pop Quigley still gets in, remember him? — the old-timers pester me to fix the dump up, but it's the damnedest thing. *This* kind threaten to leave if I touch a hair of it. I been discovered or some damn thing. Can you explain it?"

"Have you ever heard of camp?"

"No. Wait, I did hear somebody talking about it the other day, come to think of it. Couple gazebos in pink shirts. What is it?"

"Nothing. Some other time. I don't feel up to explaining it tonight." I gave a cavernous yawn. "I must get back to my party. Oh, by the way. I notice you've got the soup du jour today, Feeley. That's always been one of my favorites."

But he was in no mood for the old quips, or he had no

time for them, even if he'd heard me. He returned to the task of clattering up some old fashioneds for the gabardine. "Yeah," he said in his harassed way. "Well, glad you dropped in. See you — duh — subsequently."

"You can say that again."

7

"Can anything be made of this man? Will a butterfly ever emerge from this grub, an insect from this larva?"

I walked the living room floor on my hands as Rose addressed these apostrophes to our usual invisible ceiling cherubs, the unseen tribunal asked again to offer judgment — some light on her problem please! It's an exercise I always found invigorating once mastered, not only sending the blood to the brain but flushing the sediment out of the feet, a phenomenon none the less bracing for being an old wives' superstition with no basis in fact. Moreover the inverted position is a good one from which to put into perspective a world topsy-turvy enough in the normal.

I mused, as we went through the latest of these inventories, how they were conducted without heat. They had become a familiar part of our domestic life, even a cozy one. Almost part of our *modus vivendi* as the French say. "You know more French than I do," Rose had laughed when I made that observation.

"Can a mature and reasonable individual be hammered out of these raw materials," she went on, "bricks from this straw? *Is* there any *straw*? Because we seem to be back where we started for the umpteenth time."

"Oh, I don't think it's that many."

"It seems to be the story of your life."

"That would appear to be the case," I concurs drily, carefully stalking the room on my palms. "Judging from the number of times I've heard this spiel."

"That's not what I mean and you know it. And I wish you'd stand up. It's hard to carry on a civilized discussion with someone who's upside down."

I righted myself, smoothing down my hair. After a few deep breaths I moved to recover the offensive.

"So, winding up at Feeley's again. I know I'm getting to be a born backslider, but *that* at least wasn't my engineering. I never saw anything wrong with the joint in the first place, even without being a dump fancier. I don't cotton to slumming around in my own past, you know, and resent being forced to do so by the discerning few."

"There, *that's* what you can't see, or stubbornly refuse to. The difference between your hanging out at Feeley's in the first instance, and going back to it full circle, of an evening, with gay companions. *You went there on another level.*"

"Inverted snobbishness," I nods. "I know. I understand. I guess I'm better at walking on my head physically than intellectually."

She gave a little gasp of exasperation. "If you refuse to see the difference, then in a deeper sense you have never left Feeley's. Don't you realize that it's neither the same place you went to, nor the same you that went? Can't you grasp that? Have you read the end of *Swann's Way* yet, where it is but necessary for Mme. Swann not to appear in the Bois de Boulogne for it not to exist, as the haunt the narrator seeks to revisit? No. But you understand that line from Eliot I quoted. 'The end of all our exploring will be to arrive where we started and know the place for the first time.' "

"And it won't be the last, you can bet your sweet caboose on that."

"Gawd," she said, rolling her Mediterranean eyes.

"Maybe part of my problem is exactly this pedagogical tone you keep taking, though it must be ten years since I flunked your course. You know I love you," I snarled, "but it's a hell of a hazard to feel you're being graded every time you open your mouth or pick up a spoon. I don't know why you took exception to my calling Salisbury steak hamburger with delusions of grandeur. Both Herpolsheimers laughed."

"Glancing at each other as they did."

"So what kind of mark are you giving me as a husband so far?"

"Oh, cut it out."

"Come on, tell me. You mock your pedagogy while still meaning it, like a sponsor kidding the product. Oh, that device! So let's have it, my midsemester mark."

"You're hurting me."

"I'm only joking. So go on, give me a grade. What do I get?"

"Please."

"What do I get?"

"An incomplete."

"There, you see? It's in you." I kissed her and resumed pacing the room, right side up. This was not the time to begin the next step in my stunt: trying to walk on my head with my hands in my shoes. "I know I myself waver, between being a feather in your cap and a thorn in your side. You saw a potential possibility in me," I went on, figuring a little tautology would buck the old girl up, "and on balance I've failed you I know. Morally, socially, and now I'm not sure the same thing won't happen professionally. In the breadwinning sphere."

"What do you mean?" she asked, apprehensively.

"Nothing came of a job with Tremayne's firm. I fitted in all too well with where he took us. To him a joint like Feeley's is 'wonderful,' but wonderfulness he's not about to hire at the office. You don't want it underfoot all day. So I'm stuck batting out blurbs for rock releases at Peerless — which as you know is going under if we don't get some flapjacks in the jukeboxes pretty damn soon, to say nothing of a few on the Top Twenty. The deejays don't seem to spin us either." I shrugged reassuringly. "But I'll get something else. And meanwhile I can always go back to housekeeping."

"Why, have you seen the woman next door?"

"That's for me to know and you to find out," I says with what she called my confiding grin. "I did get a load of the six-foot-four husband, and he's not about to dig the civilized flexibility we're erecting on the rubble of Puritanism. At least I don't scream about how hard it is, housework. I'm not one of your housewives who go around with a pedometer in their pocket to show how many miles they clock in a day. How would you like to be married to somebody like that? . . . Well, are we going to church? If we're going to make the scene we'd better get dressed."

This was the evening caper, with another of the communions with which we were having, these days, an outspoken little Chateauneuf-du-Pape. It was nearing Christmas, and by coincidence Shorty took as the text for his sermon another poem of Eliot's, *The Journey of the Magi*. "A cold coming we had of it . . ." and so on. Till the end of the poem where we see this one Magi's puzzled feeling that they had witnessed a Death as well as a Birth. You probably remember it well. All right. Shorty opens with a story of how Eliot, boarding the plane to go to Stockholm for the Nobel prize ceremony, was asked by a reporter for what poem, or book, the award was being given, and Eliot called over his shoulder as he went up the stairs, "I think it's for the entire corpus." "Can't you just see this half-assed reporter, dearly beloved, combing Eliot's work for something entitled *The Entire Corpus?* Maybe a murder mystery?" All right. But then there were ominous notes of the kind that had been creeping into Shorty's messages of late, about the historicity of Christ, and even that there might be a God. We began to give each other concerned looks. Shorty went from the "text" to Eliot's essay on Virgil, who seemed to have prophesied the coming of Christ in the year 40 B.C. in something called the fourth Eclogue that I don't believe I'm familiar with, a passage of which apparently has parallels with Isaiah and what not, according to those who know. It was all pretty much over my head of course. But not the fact that Shorty was beginning to pipe a different tune from "Since nothing is certain, believe anything you want." There were some of us who feared for Shorty — that he was going to be converted. If that happened, he would be washed up as a minister. At least in these parts, among enlightened people like us. Bible banging and tub-thumping just wouldn't go down here.

But I was having occupational problems of my own those days, as I say. They began to heat up with the reappearance, in my life, of one who had temporarily dropped out of it. This was again none other than my esteemed old acquaintance, The Stopped Up Sink.

The Stopped Up Sink had left the church job as musical director, and now turned up as vocalist for a group who called themselves The Measles. We did an album of theirs after a stir they created at a Massachusetts rock festival — well named judging from the goose eggs on the heads of some who survived the riots that climaxed it, the result of mineral goodies chucked by musical devotees at the cops and even one another. The Measles had no standard uniform but were variously dressed. "Be yourself" was their principle. So one Measle sported a house painter's outfit, another was dressed as a railroad worker, complete with canvas gloves and sweat neckerchief. The album was so-so, except for the two sock numbers they'd done at the festival. Lyrics of course unintelligible, unless you followed the printed version on the back of the sleeve. The front of it pictured the four of them in their getups, with a nude reclining at their feet. This deal was a winding highway named Delilah Wells, who was having some vogue just then as a *Playboy* centerfold. She was a creamy blonde who looked as though she might have been conceived with a pastry chef's gun. It was while trying to dream up some copy for the album that an idea for a song of my own hit me and simply carried me away. *Centerfold Baby* was its title. Inspiration for several verses burning to be written seized me from time to time in company hours:

> *Centerfold cutie,*
> *Must you be so snooty,*
> *Centerfold cutie with me hee-hee,*
> *Centerfold angel with me.*
> *Here beneath the summer stars*

Let me see those staple scars.
Don't think me just a playboy,
Just a making hayboy,
Oh Centerfold baby
Say it won't be maybe,
'Cause I think I'm gonna fold over you hoo-hoo
I think I'm gonna flip over you!

It was the first time I was ever bitten by the bug to write my own songs, and the birth of that passion naturally revived my all but forgotten ambition to be a singer. I diddled doggedly with a number of tunes, trying to coax a good melody from the piano, like a trout from a stream. So half a dozen original airs were in orbit in my head the night before Christmas when a bunch of us from the church went out carolling. It was only after we'd serenaded several houses that I got into the spirit of things and forgot my own problem. Beaming goodfolk brought eggnog and mulled claret out to us in the gently falling snow. By eleven o'clock we were pretty mellowed up, with a minority getting to be three sheets, and as a result began to broaden our repertory a little. At one point we seemed to be standing in front of a bungalow blazing with colored lights singing choruses of *Buffalo Gals*. The snow was now falling thickly, and we laughed convivially within our caps and mufflers as we belted out:

> *Buffalo gals, ain'tcha comin' out tonight,*
> *Comin' out tonight, comin' out tonight.*

> *Buffalo gals, ain'tcha comin' out tonight,*
> *And dance by the light of the moon?*

Our cheeks were not as flushed as those of a short, bull-necked man who suddenly appeared in the doorway, however.

"This is the birth of our Lord, for Christ's sake!" he said. He was clutching a newspaper, and a bolt of light from a hallway fixture behind him illumined his bald head, oddly like a halo. A shiny new Oldsmobile stood in the driveway, perhaps a Holiday family present? "If you can't think of anything more fitting to sing on it than *Buffalo Gals* then go and do it somewhere else. I won't have it in front of my house." He slammed the door with a vehemence that knocked a holly wreath off it.

There wasn't anything irreverent in our mood of course, at least any intended, just a natural spillover of emotions pretty much glutted on *Silent Night* and rich drinks and fruitcake both. There are said to be a lot of suicides in the Yuletide days, quite understandable as a sort of fatal overdose of feelings, a gorge of childhood memories and indigestible make-believe, a stew of myth and escape that makes real life all the worse for our having wallowed in it. It's a hysteria to be got through, like a fit of rage, or a crying jag — or laughing. One of Rose's.

I was chuckling to myself as we rollicked off arm-in-arm down the street. Because I had the tune to *Center-*

fold Baby. One that seemed to have sorted itself magically out of the jumble of melodies sacred and secular jangling around in my head. It was now the lyrics that became the problem. None of the verses I had so far concocted fitted this particular air. So I had to start over from scratch. I fussed with lines night and day — and at work. I just couldn't get my mind on blurb copy, either for The Measles album or any others piling up on my desk. My boss, a redhead named McChesney, kept needling me about them, and one day I got back from lunch with a paper napkin in my pocket tattered with pencilled revisions to see him waiting in my office, a sheaf of lyric drafts clutched in his hand. The sight reminded me of the good man in the bungalow doorway blowing his stack over *Buffalo Gals.*

"So this is what you do on office time," he said, loud enough for his own superiors to hear *he* at least was on the job. "No wonder Manufacturing is backed up waiting for your goddamned copy, Banghart. Now hear this." He was dangerously flushed, his round red nose looking more than ever like an Exit bulb someone had screwed into the exact center of his face for a gag. "If you don't have three blurbs ready to go by five o'clock this afternoon, you don't have to bother coming back tomorrow morning. That's all, Banghart."

Getting the sack there meant less to me than it would have if I hadn't known Peerless was on the skids itself. It was like being kicked off a sinking ship, thereby being spared the bother of jumping. Peerless was taken over by another recording outfit which absorbed our office staff into theirs with a lot of streamlining I probably wouldn't have survived anyway.

For a period then I went back to door-to-door selling. All the sales techniques I had developed the first time around — the speech defect, the limp — came back to me quite naturally, along with another device I perfected for enlisting sympathy. I pretended I was an immigrant struggling to get a foothold in this great land I wanted so much to be a part of. Actually I got the idea for every one of these from salesmen who had nailed me for magazine subscriptions in the past. Until it suddenly dawned on me how agencies organizing these canvassing campaigns systematically capitalize on the moral blackmail possibilities inherent in sending these pathetic creatures stumbling and gargling up your walk. Now I was getting a little of my own back. I should have realized that eventually I was bound to strike someone with one or another of the malformations I was feigning. Still, it took me by surprise to hear a woman in a soiled housedress answer my opening splutter of vowels and consonants in kind. I wasn't selling an article then, but a service. For two dollars I would stencil people's addresses on the curbstones in front of their houses in a greenish-yellow paint that glowed in the dark, for easy reading by car callers and such. Until the police put a stop to it, I made entire blocks of Chicago streets gleam and palpitate with a sulphurous cast, if you like that sort of thing.

146

"You hay you haint hy address in whah hind of haint?" this poor creature asked after my opening salvo.

"Pho'phorehen'." It was one of those rotten breaks you extricate yourself from with as much grace as you have at your command.

"Pho'phowah?"

"Pho'phorehen'. Glows in the hark. At night. So heeple can read. 'Ook." I pointed to a job I had just done across the street. She studied it a moment, then I was relieved to see her shake her head and say she thought not today. I hobbled away, to show her there were others even more unfortunate than her in this world. But it was the last time I used defects in my sales pitches. I stayed with the deserving-foreigner act, rotating among a variety of styles: Italian, German, Spanish, and a kind of all-purpose Eastern-European speech you can't pin down to any one place. It's vaguely Balkan. "I lawv zis cawntree. I want to be good loyal American," I said. "Make living here. Becawn citizen. I study to be doctor, when I can brink poor parents over from awld cawntree, but first must work way through school. So I paint noombers on corbs so will glaw in dark for two dollars, pliz?"

I averaged about ten jobs a day, or roughly twenty dollars, sometimes a little more, but it wasn't very spiritually rewarding work, to say nothing of the physical discomfort and even danger of squatting in the gutter with my stencil and paint bucket. I took a certain pride in my skill at impersonating, at my fluent broken English. Before my change of heart, I would work elements of my repertory into different combinations, and for the day's finish, ringing the last doorbell, I would accept the supreme challenge of rolling them all into one. I would shuffle and footslap my way up the walk, a poverty-stricken orally disadvantaged immigrant gimp with parents behind the Iron Curtain, willing to do anything to earn an honest dollar. But I wasn't getting anywhere. I wasn't making something of myself. I didn't know who I was — as I had once briefly imagined I did.

It was in this frame of mind that I answered my own doorbell one day to find a smooth article clutching a briefcase with no speech defects or other physical handicaps, certainly no relatives behind the Iron Curtain, who asked whether I hadn't often thought I'd like to write. "How do you know you can't?" he said with a smile, and went on to relate the literary sales made by others, similarly deluded, who had taken a mail order course in English composition which he was selling. I agreed to take the aptitude test to which this outfit conscientiously subjected all applicants, passed it with flying colors, and enrolled in a series of lessons in fiction writing.

I didn't tell Rose that I had done so, much less plunked down two hundred fish as down payment on an ultimate eight hundred, but she eventually found out, there being no way of indefinitely concealing cancelled checks and intercepting mail. The odd part was not how useless the course was but how unnecessary: there was hardly a thing my instructor told me by mail that Rose didn't in person. She read my first story, which dealt with the ever-popular subject of life among the rich and glamorous, and shook her head.

"You've got to write about what you know," she said, which was exactly what my instructor had. "What do you know about life among the upper crust? I mean for one thing you go out of your way to work in expressions like 'beau monde,' which are precisely terms such people never use. Nor do really cultured people ever say 'cultured,' or sophisticated ones 'sophisticated.' Such words would never cross their lips. You know nothing whatever of this social level."

"You're right," I said, and to correct this situation got a part-time job as a gardener on the Bingham estate, which dominated the swanky North Shore suburbs near Evanston. The Binghams owned a commercial bakery over west.

Clipping hedges and weeding flower-beds gave me a chance to eavesdrop on conversations on the patio, or to loiter near open windows through which drifted the sound of those being conducted inside, where some of the most fashionable subjects of the hour were discussed, on sophisticated levels I'd otherwise never have been privileged to observe at such very close range: anti-heroes, environmental degradation, penis envy. I would sometimes lurk on all fours behind a bush, absolutely motionless for indefinite stretches like a lizard, taking everything in. One weekend toward the end of August I worked around the clock helping build a temporary stage for an outdoor party where the guests were to be entertained by a ballet troupe performing an original piece by a local artist whose work interpreted scenes in the American grain. Some of us menials were allowed to peer through the shrubbery at the premiere of this work, entitled *Iowa Suite,* in which farmboys pursued girls through the tall corn while dancers typifying old women shuffled about in a manner intended to depict the near-exhaustion of the lead mines near Dubuque.

In the end I saw little I could turn to literary account here, or at the bakery to which the Binghams shunted me come autumn, when no more landscaping help was needed at the estate. I was given some janitorial work there. All this time I continued writing in my spare time, working on a story with another subject altogether. This was the vastly different, but equally popular, theme of the whore with a heart of gold.

Rose shook her head after reading that one too, as my correspondence teacher had by mail.

"Again, you're not writing about what you *know,*" she said. "What do you know about prostitutes or prostitution, any more than you do about the smart set? Name me one thing."

"You're right," I said morosely, and put on my hat and went out for a walk.

I shuffled along, hands in my pockets, for block after block, thinking my problem through. I turned right up Division Street, then doubled back along a side street for three or four blocks before realizing that I had been, half-consciously, heading for a place known as a house of ill repute. It was a tavern called the All Hours Club.

The name burned in red neon script in a sign jutting out over the sidewalk between the two floors of a building shingled in fake brick, across the front of the second of which was a row of three windows with drawn shades edged with slivers of muffled light. I stood across the street watching it for some time. Dim shapes could be seen moving around the bar or huddled over it watching television, the flickering gray-green glow of which was at once the ghostliest and most definite thing in the scene. Music that couldn't possibly have had anything to do with that ectoplasm started up — a jukebox. *Mexicali Rose*. I crossed the street and went in.

Bars have made us insessorial — the term for birds that perch. It was one of the many, many words I learned while looking up others Rose used, and was able to spring in return on her. Serendipity. Five or six of us sat hunched in a semicircle like fowl silently killing time on a wet promontory over whose rocks the jukebox boomed like a steady surf from the long back room where other land birds, blown by winds to quarters not their natural habitat, nestled in wooden coves, some billing preparatory to mating elsewhere, most just sitting there like us, huddled in their ruffled feathers, in the monotonous musical spray. I downed three quick whiskeys to brace myself for maneuvers on a shore alien to me for more reasons than one. By that time a sailor in a pea jacket had asked the bartender, "How's Mother Carrie?" and been told, "Upstairs with all her chickens," without the speaker taking his eyes off a television drama of which the words were drowned out by the jukebox, so that it was like looking at a silent movie with a largely irrelevant musical accompaniment, typical of these days. Two minutes after the sailor had vanished into the back depths of the joint a middle-aged man in a brown tweed coat finished off his beer and conducted the same exchange with the bartender, then himself melted into that blatant dusk. By now I knew I had overheard the password and countersign. Not that they made much secret of them. Anyway this was it. I had one more quick one, then sidled around to the other end of the bar where the bartender was wiping glasses as he watched his program, asked with my eye also on the set, "How's Mother Carrie?" "Upstairs with her chickens."

I walked between flanking booths toward a curtained doorway through which I had seen my predecessors disappear. Beyond it at the end of a short passage was a stairway which I mounted to a locked door. I stood before it irresolutely for two or three minutes, straining to catch any noises beyond it. But the billows from the jukebox below drowned out any sounds but a scrap or two — a word here and there, footsteps, a door softly closing. I squatted to peer into the keyhole but saw nothing. There was a key in it. I stood there a while longer, reviewing my thinking and summarizing my position. I was here only as an observer, come to familiarize himself with the environment. I had no intention of becoming a patron, or doing anything above and beyond the research necessary to make my work authentic. I had this thoroughly drilled into my head when I heard footsteps definitely approaching from the other side, and knocked.

The key turned in the lock and the door was opened by a six-foot bruiser in a turtleneck sweater with a dented nose. "Yeah?" he said, as the sailor slipped past me with his head down.

"How's Mother Carrie?" I smiles. "I just wanted to see how she and all her chickens were."

"Twenty-five bucks," he said as he beckoned me in with a jerk of his head.

I shelled out the money and was led on into a big but characterless sort of parlor, or waiting room, where four girls in feathery negligées sat around under lamps with gaudy shades but dim bulbs, giving wickedness an air of strangled gaiety. The scene agreed very little with the "opulently appointed" whorehouses I had read about in books and seen in the movies, very little indeed. Where the hell were the plush sofas and gilt walls and velvet hangings, to say nothing of popping champagne corks and streams of ribald laughter? Where did the authors who gave us that impression get that stuff? Those busters certainly couldn't have done their home-work if this was any sample. Well, I would do mine. I sat down, ordered a drink from the bruiser who also ran a small bar there, and chatted for a bit with the girls.

There was a stable of eight, and I'm sure I saw all of them in the course of the quarter-hour rotations, strictly clocked by the bruiser who went around rapping on the hallway doors calling "Time's up!" as the last of his chores, but there were usually three or four on hand at a time to take your pick from (unless you wished to wait for the return of one momentarily engaged). What I was looking for was a girl who might say the words which formed the punchline that was the keystone in the story I was trying to get right. It had to do with a streetwalker fighting the forces of syndication. She liked to choose her clients, not have them choose her, was the gist of the problem, the theme. There was her pride, not to be broken in spite of humiliations or whatever storms buffeted her. She would show this in the line delivered at a crucial point. "I don't," she would say, drawing herself up to her full height and haughtily wrapping herself in her kimono, "prostitute my talent." That was the payeroo. I naturally watched for a girl with that sort of trait, in addition to a heart of gold, to select and familiarize myself with as a means of enriching my characterization — for I had reluctantly decided I would actually have to go in with one so I could get to know her a little, as well as learn something about procedures and processes. Without going whole hog, of course. That wouldn't be necessary to take in the environmental side, even fully.

There was a short redhead named Doreen in an apple-green silk wrapper, rather vivacious in a crisp, wise-cracking way. Suzette was almost her exact blonde physical counterpart. There was a coffee-and-cream Negress in a red belly-dancer outfit, who moved around a lot to show off her voluptuous figure, and a tall, statuesque brunette who kind of sat in a corner smoldering. There was an aloofness about her that on closer inspection might turn out to be pride, but was there a soft heart beating beneath that shell? I doubted it. In fact none of them seemed to have hearts of gold — until they learned I was a writer. Then they all sort of opened up and made over me. The questions tumbled out. Where did I get my ideas, what was a writer's life like, what were my hours, my working habits. Did I know any other celebrities. Did I have to be inspired. Several other customers had trickled in and out by this time, but two of them stayed to join in the conversation of which I was now the well-lubricated center. One was a rather fat salesman on a stopover, who said his wife tried to write articles and had sold one to a pet magazine on how to name an animal. "Her advice is to wait until the cat or dog has had time to establish its personality, then give it a name to suit it — don't rush into things," he said, winking at Suzette. He finally picked her and went down the hall, leaving the other participant in the literary discussion, a thin old character in a suit much too big for him, who said a friend of his once broke his leg near John P. Marquand's house. This geezer made off with a chubby woman named Estelle, leaving me to make my selection from the remaining four, and soon, because the bruiser was getting impatient over the way I dawdled, even with the round of drinks I ordered for the house, at another thirty bucks. I wasn't satisfied I had found the ideal for my story, actually a sort of Claire Trevor type, the movie actress? Worldly-wise, knowledgeable, even hard-bitten, but sympathetic withal and capable of absolute loyalty. I finally picked the redhead

Doreen, who had seemed, on balance, the most outgoing and responsive of the lot. She wanted to know *everything* about my profession, and it flatters a man to be quizzed about that.

"How long does it take you to write a book?" she asked as she unzipped in the cubicle to which she led me.

"Depends. Sometimes a year, sometimes two. Some chapters write themselves, others you sweat blood over," I said, quoting from an interview with a novelist I remembered. "But tell me about yourself. How long have you been in this?"

"Since I was twenty-two, and I'm twenty-five now. Men seem to want your life story as much as your body, why? But there ain't time for both, and you better start undressing if you want your money's worth before Nick bangs on the door. I had another intellectual in here one night, like you, only a musician, and he noticed Nick always gave four raps on the door that were like the opening of a symphony by Beethoven that's supposed to be Fate knocking on the door — da da da *da!* There, hear it? He just knocked on Suzette's. Do you know what symphony that is?"

"I can check into it. Why does he use a stick?"

"I don't know. Let's get to your stick."

"Oh, really, I . . ."

"Here, lie down. I'll do the honors."

I saw nothing wrong with letting her unbutton my clothes, as a means of glimpsing something of her skills and methods, her wiles, one thing and another, a few personal touches seen close up to lend authenticity, while she chattered on, wetting her full red lips when they weren't tightened into a concentrated circle as she squeezed a shirt-button through or struggled with my necktie. There was no harm in it whatever as long as there was no intention of going whole hog. As long as that plan was being strictly adhered to.

There was little danger it was not, judging from my condition as we stretched out naked together side by side. I "gat no heat," as the Old Testament writers put King David's similar predicament. Those Biblical busters sure could turn a phrase, to say nothing of slipping you the right remedy for a spot of trouble. The devout will remember how instead of packing the afflicted monarch off to a geriatrist or psychiatrist at twenty measures of barley a throw, why, they just popped a young girl between the sheets with him. Precisely the treatment here. For what have we, what is this, going to lengths we had not anticipated through no fault of our own? I experienced something of the delicate ministrations and persuasions of which these artists in the act of love are capable, so much so that, as she softly breathed "Come on baby," into my ear, "That's the boy, ah, now there we are," and such like encouragements, I found myself helpless in her encircling arms, then being gently cajoled over onto her as she spread her freckled pink legs in welcome, all of me save the member she daintily caressed now a defenseless pulp, a dissolving jelly of bliss, then, much too late, felt myself sink into her. The very marrow of my bones seemed to be sucked out through my loins into hers, which dutifully writhed

157

and heaved themselves in a response I knew was as simulated as my salesman's limp, but, even so, appreciated as an accomplished part of the service delivered. She exhaled a long and quivering sigh like mine, and I parted from her flesh and fell back, spent, upon the bed just as the four beats sounded on the door. "Time's up!"

"Can I see you sometime?" I asked, dressing.

"I'm here any night after seven."

"I mean during the day."

She paused in her own dressing and looked at me dubiously. With a slowly dawning expression of pleased surprise, like a child's, she said, "Well, sure. If you want. I live in that big corner apartment building. I'll give you my phone number if you've got a pencil. You're different."

There was no shortage of local color or authentic detail about the way of life I was researching in the days that followed. Because I was suddenly seized by the fear that I might have picked up a nail. Once the thought got its hooks into me, nail enough, I could hardly put word to paper for running into the bathroom every five minutes to see if there were any developments. Sometimes I sat at the typewriter with the damned thing hanging out in my lap, for quick spot-checks between bursts of gunfire. The stimuli great writers have depended on to get the creative ball rolling is always interesting. There was a little article about that in the magazine published by my mail-order school. Shelley subjected his head to heat in order to get turned on. Just how or what kind was not specified, whether he put it in an oven for a few minutes, or swaddled it in a hot towel or what. Heine laid down on a couch for a while (not a stimulus really, but a composing of the mind). Housman drank beer, de la Mare needed tobacco to get going, Hart Crane liquor and jazz music, Schiller the smell of rotten apples. God knows what I was writing smelled bad enough, thus one paragraph sent me on to the next.

No burning on urination the first day or two, or the third, but the fourth — wasn't that a slight sting accompanying the last of the outgoing dregs? What a sordid business at a time of great virtue — for it goes without saying that I now underwent a moral rebirth that made the others look like lapses from grace. This was all-out. I mean a basic reaffirmation of values. From fearing to drink water so as to avoid the test I went to gulping down quarts of it to keep the test moving, purchasing with each trip another twenty minutes of reprieve. Why not take notes on *that*, on the pangs of remorse while they're still fresh in the mind? Impossible. Too close to the subject. Perhaps the physical stinging was imaginary, a product of my overwrought imagination. Of course! Pshaw! The fifth day came and went. Wasn't I off the hook now? I hotfooted it to the local library and sat down in a corner of the reference room with a medical encyclopedia. Hunched over it, an arm cupping it to shield it from witnesses, a finger in another section ready to flip the pages over in case anyone did stop by, I read what it had to say. ". . . appears usually within a period of five to eight days after exposure." Eight days! Three more of this bed of spikes before going on to that other rack — No, don't say it. Yes, face it. Don't look up *those* symptoms now, oh God, but realize it'll be next on the agenda. Three more days of wrestling with this monster before going on to that twin whose name we know.

Every hypochondriac is a medical student. I had become the one overnight and therefore the other. I became an expert not only on diagnosis but on the larger issue of public health. The VD rate is away up again, we've got to do something about it. An informed citizenry is our only hope — an informed and aroused one. I also read newspaper accounts of some recent crackdowns on prostitution. In Washington, D.C., and some other cities, undercover policewomen posing as streetlamp solicitors snared and booked all male customers with the aid of cops lurking in nearby squad cars. Which strikes me as rather dirty pool.

Off the one hook, I went on to my really big homework.

It was by chance mid-afternoon, and there was the usual cluster of high-school girls buzzing around the reference shelves in the library, or sitting at the tables copying out notes, their long hair hanging from their inclined heads, their ripe loins warming the seats. Oh, how I would like to be looking up osmosis, or the Punic Wars, or the chief products of Venezuela! Their collective fragrance was an air blown from that Garden from which I was now banished — for who would chance making love to his wife while this was hanging fire? I have used the word chance twice within almost as few lines: symbol of my obsession. Because every time the word shot off a page at me, or I heard it from someone's lips, my tormented mind automatically slipped an 'r' in between the last two letters. When might that little old rosebud first be expected to appear? I snatched the medical manual off the shelf, found the last vacant chair, and gobbled down the facts.

"Tradition has it that . . . acquired by Columbus's sailors from the Indian maidens in America and introduced to Europe . . ." Never mind the importers, let's get to the essentials. "The French called it the Italian disease, and the Italians called it . . ." We *know* all that. Skip the comic relief, shall we? We're in no mood. "The cause is an animal parasite, the spirochaeta pallida . . . After infection the disease itself is usually divided into three stages. The first is signalled by the appearance of a chancre, which forms at the point of entrance of the causative organism. It forms about six weeks after inoculation." Six weeks! Five more in this frying pan? No, I'm sorry. Two more is my limit, maybe three at the outside, that's my last offer. But what's this next little tidbit? "By the time the chancre forms, the spirochaeta has spread to all parts of the body."

It had not been my impression on passing the desk where the librarian Mrs. Bodne sat that her dress was polka dotted. Yet now her fat bulk seemed covered with these dark spots, swimming before my eyes. Other occupants of the room appeared similarly clad, even the men. Also they had since last glimpsed a few seconds ago contracted measles? To a person. The room itself began to sway, to melt like a structure in a surrealist film, growing dimmer as I lowered my head on down to my arm. Some protective instinct made me close the volume so packed with informational goodies as I did so, so no one coming to my rescue would get a gander at what I was curled up with. Not a good Samaritan showed up, however, as I was glad to see when I came to what must have been only a minute or two later.

That was enough for one day without some self-administered first aid though. I put the manual back on the shelf and slipped across the street for a little of the old liquid lobotomy. Even in the kindly dusk of the bar mirror my face looked like something carved out of frozen manure. My memory churned up things I had heard or read in the past about Subject A, to augment what I'd just picked up. Fathers who walked "funny" to the kitchen in grim novels depicting the destruction of entire families on which their sins were visited. Yes, locomotor ataxia was one of the vivider by-products all right. You thought of remittance men in out-of-the-way tropical holes hardly able to put one foot in front of another long enough to pick up at the local post office the checks their people sent them to keep them out of sight. Then what was "saddle nose" again? Didn't that come along in the third stage when the bones were eaten away —? I drank off a third whiskey and scuttled on back to the library to get it over with.

The words that slithered up at me off the page this

time were only a nastier nest of reptiles than the first. "In the second stage . . . general eruption . . . hair may fall out . . . Tertiary stage includes all the late manifestations . . . breaking down of tissue . . . liver, bones, meningeal covering of the brain . . . locomotor ataxia . . . and, in its final ravages, the form of insanity known as paresis. This . . ."

I tottered down the library steps, scarcely able to put one foot in front of another. *Already?* You got it, Jack. This is a galloping case. I definitely walked "funny" back to the bar, the wet edge of which I gripped in nerveless fingers to supplement what little strength remained in the rubber legs on which I stood. I averted my eyes from the mirror for fear of finding that a concavity had begun to form across the bridge of my nose. My tongue patrolled the inside of my mouth for the "mucous patches" and other lesions celebrated in the little delectation to which I had just treated myself. Two or three more belts of the old chloroform, instead of relaxing me, only seemed to offer a warm breeding ground for the vipers proliferating steadily in my head. I slept badly, dreamed all manner of muck, and awoke with a mold on my tongue an inch thick. I scoured it off with my toothbrush, scrubbing away until I gagged. My eyes were like blood blisters.

This couldn't go on. Toward the end of the fourth week, taking the thousandth gingerly gander at the old stem, I thought I noticed a small pink spot near the tip. A chill of horror ran up my spine. Could this be the real thing, or just a product of all the investigatory clawing and mauling the poor creature had taken? I searched my arms and face for little dermatological nothings it could be shown to resemble. It had the white spot in the center common to a lot of these garden-variety pimples. But it didn't go away, in fact it grew. It was time to go see a doctor.

That I hadn't done so before and settled all this *Schrecklichkeit* one way or another was due to one thing. My understanding that a physician had to report every case of social disease (what a name!) to the public health authorities, who would naturally keep tabs on you, probably with follow-up calls at your house. I was stewing about this when I happened to pass a vet's. He surely wouldn't be required by law to report you, while having enough medical savvy to evaluate your situation. On a distracted impulse I went up the short walk to his door. It stood open, beside a shingle reading: Gomer Beansod, D.V.M.

The name was ominous enough. It dissolved any remaining doubts. I knew as I went through that door that I had clap and syphilis both — the one late blooming, the other already tooling along toward its terminal stage. Foreboding too were the sounds that greeted me in the empty waiting room: shrieks and howls and barks and yelps from the other patients, coming through the consulting room from the kennels and hutches beyond. The consulting room was empty too, I could see when I poked my head into it through an open door. I wandered all the way in, crossing to the door that led out to the grounds where the kennels were. The whole place seemed deserted, as though everybody around had fled, or maybe been devoured by the clamoring beasts in a general uprising. A couple of minutes passed. Then the animal sounds subsided, and I heard a voice coming through a back wall, from what was obviously the doctor's living quarters. I picked up a stethoscope, and holding the bell, or whatever they call it, to the wall, I tried to pick up what seemed one end of a telephone conversation. A woman, undoubtedly Mrs. Beansod, was chatting with what had to be another woman. She had a low voice, and laughed a lot, though nervously it struck me, not with much mirth.

". . . to do but sweat it out. Oh, that may be too strong a term — no, it isn't, not when you're being put up for the Cedarbrook Country Club. The Bagshaws are sponsoring us and we've got two seconds, I won't say who they are, but only one carries any real weight there. With only three openings — thuree — for eighteen applicants, Agnes, I just don't know. It's touch and go. Gome has his heart set on it, both for the golf and the social reasons, and I don't know what we'll do if we don't get in. Hang our heads in . . ."

"Yes?"

I turned around. In the doorway leading to the kennels — where the Hounds of the Baskervilles were tuning up again — stood a short bald man with intense brown eyes, wearing a white duster in the pockets of which his fingers chewed on something — money, keys, implements. This was not a family with an air of repose about it. These people needed help. I removed and dropped the stethoscope on a table, pinching my eyes and the bridge of my nose with the kind of sigh by which professional people tell you they are having a rough day.

"Dr. Beansod?"

"Yes. What can I do for you?"

"My request is a rather unusual one," I said. "My problem is a rather special one — though far, far from unheard of. To come to the point — Cigarette?"

"No, thanks."

"I smoke three packs of these a day — and I don't smoke." I lit the cigarette with a match I finally had to put into my pocket, there being no ashtray around. I let it go out in my hand after a few drags. "That'll give you some idea of the state of mind I'm in. To come to the point, I've been with a woman I have some doubts about, and I'm afraid I may have a souvenir. I don't want to go to my doctor for obvious reasons, and to another for the same ones. I was wondering if you'd take a look at it. If you'd do me that favor. Extend me that courtesy," I went on in the silence during which he simply looked at me.

"I'm only a veterinarian."

"You are too modest. You underestimate the value of that calling. We're all God's creatures, and to draw fine distinctions —"

"And my patients don't get themselves into scrapes like that," he added with a rather smug little smile. I was finding this an intolerant sort of customer, as well as uptight. "In any case, I don't have a license to practise

166

that kind of medicine. If one of us goes to prison, or ends up in disgrace, I'd prefer it were you."

Dr. Beansod had all this while been conducting his half of the conversation from the doorway, holding the screen partly open behind him. He let that go and entered the room, brushing past me toward the other side. He began to poke about among some bottles and tubes on a shelf, his back to me.

"I'm not asking you to look at it as a doctor. Only as a friend."

"But I don't know you."

"Then as a stranger. A private citizen — a plain human being! Is that too much to ask?"

"I'm afraid my answer is final. Now if you'll excuse me, I have things to do." He drew on a pair of steel-rimmed spectacles that gave him an even more tense and removed air, hooking them first onto one ear, then the other, in a puttery way like an old man, though he couldn't have been more than forty.

"Do you know what a *cri de coeur* is?"

"I am familiar with lesions and pathologies common to animals. Those contracted by people, under circumstances that are their own business, are not my province," he said, acquiring more and more the manner of a lofty intellectual.

"Couldn't you just look at it? Just the merest glance, to get a man off the hook. A fellow human being, one with a wife and five children," I bleated. "It may be just a pimple. Shucks, here, let me just —"

"Don't you dare take that thing out in here!" he exclaimed in actual panic. "One look and it's malpractice. Do you hear me! A vet gets these things constantly, people come in with pets, and while they're being treated they'll ask your opinion on, oh, a mole, a possibly infected finger of their own. Just casually. Incidentally. Obviously we have many things in common with animals, and a word of comment murmured in passing might be perfectly harmless, but one can't take that chance!" There was that damned word again! "The other day I refused to look at a wart on a woman's chin. It sounds rigid, but I simply can't have it. Not in here."

"All right, let's go outside. I'll tell you what." I walked to a window and peered out of it, shading my eyes with my hands. "How about that garage out there?"

"Never!"

"There seems to be some kind of supply room, or toolshed, next to it. We could step into there a minute."

"Will you please go?" He dropped his head and, lifting the glasses a little with thumb and forefinger, pinched his eyes in a weary gesture plagiarized from my own. I breathed a long sigh together with his. I watched him readjust the specs and then proceed to pour something from a bottle into a measured beaker. He interrupted this to put some surgical or examining instruments into a sterilizer.

"Dr. Beansod, I think you'll look at this thing," I said quietly.

"Mister, I don't think I will."

"Dr. Beansod, I think you will when you hear what I have to say."

He paused and studied me speculatively over his shoulder, arrested by something in my manner. He returned to his work, though all ears I could tell.

"I happen to know that you and Mrs. Beansod are trying to get into the Cedarbrook Country Club. And also what it means to you. We both also know it's touch and go at best — what with the waiting list? I happen to be a member, and what's more, high in the councils of — well, we don't ourselves use the term desirable element, or establishment, but there you have it. I could use my influence."

He turned around, paling. "You mean you'd try and queer —"

"Come, come," I said. "Do I look like the kind who'd resort to blackmail?"

"You, sir, are a cur."

"Then I've come to the right place," I said, smiling as patiently as I could. "No, Doctor, I am talking about the exact reverse of blackmail — helping a fellow human being up the social ladder. If you refuse my simple little request" — I shrugged — "I'll go my way and forget about you, as you will me."

"Hardly!"

"But if you give me a break, I'll reciprocate. You know what red tape is, and that it's never unwound — just cut. I happen to know the chairman of the membership committee. In fact he's a close friend of mine."

His expression softened, and some of the color seeped back into his cheeks.

"It would practically cinch it. You know how those

things go. Pull is everything. A word, a name dropped into the right ear over cocktails, and the whole thing is settled."

He resumed his work with his back to me.

"If I did such a favor for a friend in here, it would be malpractice, as I say."

"It's a big city. There's the park. It's only a minute. You could be right back."

"The fact of the matter is I have to go that way to a business appointment. My office hours are over for the day. This other matter apart, I'd like to talk to you about the club. How those things work. I don't know what my wife will do if we don't make it. Probably have a nervous collapse. You know how those things are."

"Of course," I said, sympathetically. "The struggle for status, a place in the sun. I understand. Well, why don't you meet me in front of the park in, say, ten minutes."

I was waiting for Dr. Beansod there when he arrived, wearing a blue jacket for the professional tunic, together with gray checked trousers and a tweed hat that gave him a sporty look. We strolled up one of the gravel walks looking for an unoccupied bench.

"Lovely weather we've been having," I said.

"How long have you known Eddy?"

"Eddy who?"

"James Eddy. Chairman of the membership committee."

"Oh, that Eddy. Not very long. To be absolutely frank with you, it's Jack Pinkerton I'm close to, on that committee, but Eddy's getting on now, and he takes all his cues from Jack, especially on the new element we're getting in there, the more snappy set." I gave Beansod an admiring glance. "Which you certainly answer to."

We made for an empty bench in a relatively deserted section of the park. We sat on it for a bit, chatting about the club and its inner workings. Then he drew up a cuff to consult his wristwatch. "I should be going or I'll be late for my appointment." He glanced around. "Shall we get this over with?"

"Want to go in the bushes?"

"Good Lord no. No need for anything that suspicious-looking. There's nobody around right now, so hurry."

While he darted furtive looks in all directions, I straightened on the bench to draw my zipper down, fished out the mooted member, and held it in my palm for inspection. He bent down to peer at it, drawing on the steel-rimmed spectacles. I turned it a little to point to the pink spot, which, I noted with a fresh pang of apprehension, had again enlarged. After a moment, he raised his head.

"Oh, my God."

"She the real thing, Doc?"

"Don't call me *Doc!*"

"All right, all right. But what's the dope? Tell me the worst. Let me have it straight."

"I just now realized. *I* don't know what the damned things look like any more than you. How could I? I've never seen one. My patients don't turn up with them," he said, again with the touch of complacency.

171

"Oh, for God's sakes," I groaned, tucking it back in. "What did you agree to this for then? I make a bargain with you and you get me out here under false pretenses."

"You got me so mixed up I wasn't thinking."

I moaned again — not as loudly as I did a second later. A figure in a blue uniform emerged from the bushes, dropping a pair of binoculars hanging from a lanyard around his neck. A camera dangled from another thong.

"All right, that's enough of that," came in an Irish brogue as he scrambled along a short grass incline toward us. "I'll have to run you both in."

Dr. Beansod rose, his knees visibly shaking. "No, you've got this all wrong, officer. He — he —"

"That's right, officer," I said. "The fault is mine, if any. He was just sitting here by himself, and I accosted him. I never saw him before."

The cop looked at Beansod, whose face had fallen apart. "That's right. I never saw this man before in my life. Now if you'll just excuse me —"

"Just a minute. I may want a witness against him."

"You won't need that, officer. Anything you say I'll admit to. Did you get a picture?"

"No, but I —"

"It won't be necessary anyway. But I'd like to make a few accusations myself, if I may," I said, figuring I had nothing to lose any more. An odd cynical calm had taken hold of me that I could only explain as a welcome evictor of the doubt and anxiety I had been laboring under. "Or ask a few questions. What the hell is this with cops lurking in the shrubbery, with binoculars yet? Is the police force made up of voyeurs?"

"We're launching a drive on far too many fags. And other sex offenders." He turned to the ashen Beansod. "All right, you can go I guess. I can't claim to have seen you do anything out of the way. The best I could make stick is an exposure case. We need them like a hole in the head too, lately."

Beansod took off at a brisk clip. I called after him. "About the club, I'll give Jack Pinkerton a buzz —"

"No!" he cried in terror as he fled. "I don't know you! Don't mention my name to anybody. Forget you ever . . ."

The cop, a beefy blond named Murphy, walked me to a nearby callbox, where he telephoned for a squad car in which I was whisked to the Chicago Avenue Court, a district police court where I was booked on a misdemeanor and held for trial. Or maybe they call it a hearing. It amounts to a trial in any case.

Luckily the standard assortment of pimps and prostitutes and drunks was thin that day and I didn't have long to wait. In the hour or so I did hang around — feeling at last an integral part of the lower depths I had set out to study and aimed to depict, experiencing a real sense of belonging — I fell into conversation with a furtive little man in a tight-fitting suit of chalk-stripe blue who admitted he was also in for a misdemeanor but refused to say what it was. It couldn't have been his first charge, I was sure from the intimate knowledge he displayed of this level of American jurisprudence. Murphy, who lolled back yawning with boredom, leniently let me pick this customer's brains.

"This pickle I'm in," I said in a low voice, "is the result of a complete and utter misunderstanding."

If there can be such a thing as a sympathetic leer he was the master of it.

"Whole thing a ghastly mistake?" he answers, a smile contorting an all but non-existent mouth, itself even normally running in a crooked little line, like a paper-clip twisted out of shape by a nervous wreck. "It's an outrage? An injustice? They haven't heard the last of this?"

"That's right," I said, speaking out of the side of my own mouth so Murphy wouldn't hear me on the other. The guy nodded, waggling a foot on the knee of the other leg. He kept shooting his neck out of the collar of his shirt, as though it was necessary to keep his Adam's apple above the knot of his tie so it could bob freely.

"Well, I'll give you some free legal advice. The quickest way out from under an injustice — an outrage — know what I mean? — the quickest way out is to plead guilty."

"But I'm innocent."

"So plead innocent, have bail set, scrounge up the bail, hire a lawyer and be bound over for trial in a criminal court. Know what I mean? For good measure you might sue the city for false arrest and *really* get your name smeared all over the papers."

"I see what you mean. Whereas if . . ."

He tapped my knee with a tabloid he had rolled up

into a tube. "If you plead guilty and pay your fine you could be home and dry in an hour. You look like a decent sort of damn fool to me, so I won't charge you for the advice. But you goddam well better take it or you'll be sorrier tomorrow than you're sore today. Is that you being paged?"

My case was called just then and instinct told me to take his advice. The fine slapped on me was fifty bucks, which I didn't have on me, so I had to telephone Rose and ask her to come bring it and get me out of here. There was an amusing little comedy of errors which I would explain later.

"Al, where the devil have you *been?*" she asked when she heard my voice. "I've been worried stiff about you. Have you forgotten? Reverend Shorty's coming to dinner tonight."

8

Causes of things are nowhere harder to disentangle from occasions for them than in a marital relationship leading to a bustup. The occasion for the First World War was the murder of the Archduke at Sarajevo, but no one would say that was its cause, or even one of them. The cause of Rose's finally leaving me was, you might say in plain English, that she'd simply had enough. Of her rhinestone in the rough, as the agent called his actor. Confession is good for the soul, and especially good for the heel, and I again made a clean breast of things. The occasion? My promise to turn over a new leaf. "No! Not that!" she cries in a manner that reminds me of poor Dr. Beansod fleeing in terror from my promise to recommend him at the country club. Am I really that bad? I will try again. Nobody likes to be deplorable. Incidentally, I did put in a good word for him with the other pillars of society there and he did get in. I realize that my own right to swim in that pool and use those greens rests squarely on Rose Piano's translations of Racine.

Rose had been through a lot, I admitted that freely. And her position was clearly and compactly summed up. She could forgive the lecher and the poltroon (this seemed to be the last of the cumulative, or compounded, *tirades* in a drama drawing to its appointed close), she could forgive the ersatz rebel on the soapbox at the hat factory, she could forgive the philanderer, she could forgive the door-to-door schlep with his bag of tricks, she could forgive the no-talent deluding himself he had a little, and she could, and did, now, forgive the wanghouse patron whose story that he had been arrested in a raid there she could well believe, because he had already aroused her suspicions by not sleeping with her for a month. (That was the version I gave her when she came down with the fine money.) What she could not face was a fresh start leading to a whole new set of shambles.

"You can cook up more calamity than I can sit down to," she said. "I'd still stick if I thought I could do you any good. But it seems I can't. Maybe I'm bad for you. Maybe our chemistry is wrong, as they say about actors in a play that doesn't go. Anyway, Shorty needs me now.

Maybe more than you do, or even ever did. You only seem to keep winding up back where you started. He's going steadily downhill — and doesn't know it."

I knew they'd been seeing a little of each other as a result of her constant presence at a church production of another of her translations. I hadn't known it was a question of there being something between them.

"Why, what's the matter with Shorty?"

"You know. He's got religion, and that's bad in a minister. It's like a surgeon having heart. Interferes hopelessly with his work. Could he take your gall bladder out with tears in his eyes?"

I had realized what she meant. I only wanted to hear her explain it as a way of finally clarifying the problem to myself. It gave me small consolation, either for Shorty or me. I stood at the window looking gloomily into the street. "Don't let your woman's sympathy run away with your head, Rose."

"Oh, come now. You always said that's precisely the weakness you were the beneficiary of."

"I *did?*" I said, pleasantly amazed.

"Well, perhaps not in so many words."

"Now it's Shorty's turn. For a little of that gravy. I dig. I get the message."

"Look. I'm afraid he's on the verge of cracking up. He talks more and more about being 'saved,' and when people do that they tend to slip out beyond human connection — except with others like themselves. The religious psychosis is a form of insanity that's —" She laughed, shaking her head at what she was about to say.

178

"It's almost therapeutic. I read somewhere — I think it may have been in one of Iris Murdoch's novels — Did you read the one I gave you?"

I flapped out my arms, as one who despaired of himself, and asked to be shown no mercy.

"Anyway, the point one of the characters makes is this. That people often take leave of their senses on the subject of religion, who do not otherwise take leave of their senses. Sometimes a little madness in the realm of faith stabilizes the rest of the psyche. You can bear the world if you think it's just a way-station on a trip to heaven. Believing in Santa Claus will see you through the year. I don't think that's the case with Shorty. I think he's flipping, or has flipped. Something to do with some terrible guilt involving a rigid Presbyterian father. And what's worse, mother." Rose drew a sigh a yard long, sitting in a straight chair in a position I suddenly realized was typical with her. Goodbyes wake us up to things we haven't noticed. She sat with her hands behind the chair, as though she'd been tied into it by a criminal who had just broken into the house. "So if you don't mind, if you're willing to mark time with me, tread water for a bit, see what we see . . ."

"Sure. Not talk about divorce or anything like that just yet."

"No, no. Play it by ear."

"Those twin slices of smoked salmon you've got between your —"

"Don't."

Something else happened that sped her departure. A

college in Connecticut offered her a good job. She made a whirlwind trip out to case the place, liked it, and moved into a rented house in a town called Rowayton. Meanwhile Shorty lost his job at Community Church, where the gabardine had had just too much of sermons telling them to repent and come to Jesus, to get down on their knees right then and there and accept him as their Savior. This sort of thing began to escalate rapidly and alarmingly. He spread his arms, striking the cruciform position dear to these evangelists, and said, "Come unto me, all ye that labor and are heavy laden, and I will give you rest," without any sign of giving credit for the line. The gabardine looked at each other with the chills going up their spines. The central committee met in emergency session and gave Shorty a nice long vacation, with overwork offered as the reason. Rose took him east with her.

It turned out I was in good health, though that was about all you could say for me. The apartment was too big and too expensive for me to keep alone, so I put into storage the little furniture I hadn't made Rose take and moved into a rooming-house. Mrs. Krakauer was your perennial widow landlady, bustling around in a mob-cap and answering the door with a broom in her hand. She jabbered day and night about her tenants, but especially about a "mystery" lodger named Duane Decker, a stringy towhead of about twenty-five with blue eyes like a pair of shooting marbles. He kept to himself, always, I began to notice, in view of the rest of us. Mrs. Krakauer told me that he had once played the violin, but that he had put it down, never to touch it again, after suffering some kind of heartbreak.

"What kind of heartbreak?" I asked, letting myself be sucked into a bog of schmaltz because I suppose I was in the mood for it. "Was it unrequited love?"

"What kind of love?"

"Where it's not returned. You carry the torch for some broad who hands you a load of ice cubes."

Mrs. Krakauer gave her own special combination of sigh and shrug, at the same time darting around the foot of my bed which she was making, tucking in the "hospital corner" almost in passing, she had become so deft at it. I watched her from the single easy chair in the room, to which I was confining myself with a bad cold. I thought of the time when I had for a short spell made the beds with my feet, to enliven the boredom of my distaff days. How long ago they seemed!

"People can die of a broken heart," I said, just as a way of getting her to stay and rap a while, though I admitted to myself it was a matter of putting her on. I threw out these cues to keep her going, or start her up again when she showed signs of running down. She had told me that her own husband had "died of furniture moving," her way of declaring that hard work had killed him, for an outfit apparently criminally delinquent in its pension payments. I always thought of her as the Ump, ever since the evening at the kitchen table when I'd gotten her to ramble on about what she meant by the "undesirable element" she claimed her secret radar could screen out at the door with a glance. "Physically and

morally low," she said. "Many's the ones I took in knowing they might be financial risks, and carried them for
weeks at a time too, I didn't mind. And many's those I
let take a girl up to their room, or woman. *A* girl or
woman. Not girls or women. If they were their steadies,
what harm? It's the indiscriminate ones I ruled out, and
believe you me I could smell them at the door when they
applied. Slick as a whistle they might be, neat as a pin,
but you can spot something wrong. Oh, once in a while
you can make a mistake, we're none of us perfect. Once
I had a salesman in here who it turned out had the
sociable disease. When I learned that — *Out!* What's so
funny?"

I had to tell her. "What you do when you say 'Out!'
You swing your thumb over your shoulder just like an
ump calling somebody out at the plate."

"I wouldn't know. I got no time for ball games."

"Tell me more about the Bird That Sings No More," I
said this morning, seeing she was almost finished tidy-
ing up my room and wanting to keep her for a bit.
"Where did you hear this about never playing another
note since this tragedy befell him?"

"I don't know. One of the other roomers."

"Which one?"

"How do I remember? They all talk about it. What are
you, cross-examining me or something?"

"No, no. I just want to get to the bottom of it. He
fascinates me, this Duane — which is just what he
wants of course, though not exactly in this way. He's
become a legend as the result of a rumor we can't

seem to trace to its source. Maybe he started it himself,
with or without a basis in fact. That we don't know for
sure. But it does give him a special aura. Do you know
what a mythomaniac is?"

The Ump threw me a look of wild alarm. "You mean
I might be harboring a nut in the house?"

"No, no," I said, suppressing a pang of my own at
what had been another of Rose's words. "This is harmless fantasizing, they call it. People who tell fibs."

"Oh," the Ump says with relief. "Liars."

"Well, it's not that exactly. Less, and more. They
weave this whole, like, tissue of stuff about themselves,
that usually has a lot of wish fulfillment to it."

"There's a lot of that going around," said the Ump,
glancing into my wastebasket. Seeing it was empty, she
stepped into the hall for her dustmop.

"In this case it does give our Duane — and I might
add the name sounds fishy to me too — a romantic air.
The Mysterious Stranger come out of the night and
vanishing at last into the night —"

"Like Bulldog Drummond on them old radio pro-
grams!"

"— about whom nothing is really known, except this
. . . this secret grief. The Stricken Artist. It's kept de-
liberately vague, misty, so it'll be whispered about all the
more, by you, me, all of us. Now wait. Just a second. I'm
not saying it doesn't have a foundation in fact. Let's say
he did once play the violin. He fell madly in love with
this beautiful woman, who spurned him. Or maybe she
died. It's possible. But the truth itself can become an act.

183

We're all such role-players, you see. *We can make an affectation out of an actual reality.*"

"You writers," she said, rolling her eyes in pride at her clientele. "You're so deep." She clattered about under the bed with the dustmop, on all fours, as I dilated on the Bird That Sang No More.

I pointed out that he was always standing at the window gazing out alone in full view of others lounging about the front parlor, whereas if he really wanted the solitude he appeared to crave, all he had to do was stay in his room. Why bother coming down? And why was he always going for long walks in the rain? Why didn't he go out when it was dry, like the rest of us? No, he had to be the drenched poet, nursing his sorrow as he trudged alone through the wet night . . . But there are certifiable broken hearts, I reminded myself, whatever a skeptical age might think. What were those lines from Millay that Rose liked to recite? "The heart once broken is a heart no more, And is absolved from all a heart must be." I really must get to the bottom of this Duane Decker deal, I thought, watching Mrs. Krakauer close the door behind her, leaving me alone in the chair to brood. I vowed that I would. And I did. But I'll tell his story presently, at the appointed moment in my own . . . a turn of events I'd never have dreamt in a thousand years.

Two evenings later, it being a clear moonlight night, I went for a walk myself. Fascination drew me like an irresistible magnet back toward the All Hours Club.

184

After watching the place from across the street, like I had the first time, I went in. I roosted at the bar over a few beers, hearing other patrons inquire about Mother Carrie's Chickens with no desire to look in on them myself. But I was itching to see again the one I'd picked for myself that night, the little redhead Doreen. I had to admit that. I had kept her telephone number, and I finally called her the next afternoon.

"Oh, the musician!"

"No, I'm the one whose ear you bent about the musician. Remember?"

"My God, you. Of course I do. Are you writing anything lately?"

"No, I . . ." I sighed into the transmitter. "Something's happened to me. I don't think I'll ever write another line."

"Aw. Whuh hoppen?"

"I don't want to talk about it. All I do is go for long walks in the rain. You don't want me to do that, do you? Catch my death?"

"No! You're basically a sweet individual. Coming over? Taking me to lunch? What's on your mind?"

"I thought we might rip a chop."

The waif had bittersweet memories of her own, of which she unburdened her breast with her head on mine. She had once loved a ponce, in the tradition of her kind, for whom she poured out the true emotion fiercely kept from the clients he drummed up for her. That treasure from her heart of hearts was his and his alone, as it became mine when I succeeded him in her affection, as I soon did. We rushed into the void of one another's lives, each filling the other to the brim with a newfound happiness. She had a falling out with the owners of the All Hours, despotic masters trying to enslave an essentially independent spirit. One that retained its central, almost childlike, innocence through everything. I encouraged her to make a break, and she did.

"You'll have to help me then," she said, watching me as she drained off a glass of milk like the little girl she basically was. "If you agree I should do this and keep my self-respect. Not prostitute my art, like you say. You're so *deep*."

"I won't have you walking the streets, if that's what you mean."

"Then you'll have to help me. You'll have to help Doreen."

In helping her, I helped also those lonely wayfarers, the flotsam and jetsam of the night, who found a few moments' respite in her arms.

I was moving in with her little by little, by stages so gradual not even the hawk-eyed Ump could see what I was sneaking out of the rooming-house, now a shirt hidden under my coat, now a few pairs of socks in my pockets. I don't really know why I made such a secret of my departure, or what purpose I thought hoodwinking Mrs. Krakauer served. Maybe I wasn't sure this was "the real thing," so wanted to keep the move tentative or partial. One night on my rounds of bars and street corners I stopped by to pick up a topcoat, to find Mrs. Krakauer waiting up for me in the parlor.

"There's a lady in your room," she said, closing a magazine. "I refused to let her in at first, but she insisted. Certainly seems like a nice person. She says she's your wife, or used to be. I finally saw no harm . . . You sometimes have to make these quick . . ."

Rose was sitting in the window chair, reading still another magazine. She had on a crisp blue linen suit with nubs in it of a slightly paler material, the white collar of her blouse spread out over it. She set the magazine aside, smiling in greeting as she tossed her head, still shaking out hair she'd forgotten she cut.

"Hello, Al. I came back to wind up a few things. But mainly to talk to Shorty's parents, and frankly see if they can help with a little money. He's living with me, strictly on a residential basis. I couldn't take on anybody emotionally like that; I mean in that shape."

"You don't have to explain yourself, Rose. I understand." There being no other chair, I took the bed, neither sitting on it nor lying, but propped against the headboard on a wadded pillow. "Shorty's that bad, huh?"

"He waits for Christ's return every day. How are you?"

"Nothing like that. I'm living with . . ." I decided to tell her. "I'm living with the girl I visited, that time the club got raided?" Making a clean breast of untruths struck me peculiar in the circumstances, but of course the fabrications were unessential. "We mean something to each other. Good for what it is. You once said honest pennies were better than fake silver dollars, even though you passed the dollars."

"Oh, come now! She probably said it. What are you doing? I mean what kind of work."

"I help her out some."

"I see." She studied her hands, folded in her lap. "So you wind up a pimp. Well, at least you can't sink any lower."

"Don't be too sure." For I had a picture of myself in one last guise, my shoes shined, my suit pressed, swinging my briefcase from door to door as I greeted housewives with, "How do you know you can't write? Let us show you how."

I sensed her eyeing me. She now put her hands behind her back again, that is behind the chair, as though another housebreaker had tied her wrists. "You'd do anything to get a girl back, wouldn't you?" she said with the kind of tight little smile that absolutely ruled out any chance of a laughing fit.

I answered as though the remark had not been made — we were still talking about Shorty. "You've got a sign around your neck, Will Alter to Suit Tenant. Haven't you? You'll never change. Oh, let's go for a walk. We can rap better on foot, maybe."

We wandered under winter boughs through which the jaundiced light from streetlamps filtered. The talk was as aimless as our walk, though in five minutes we got in everything in a nutshell about each other. Rose was happy in her job, loving the college and her classes and most of her colleagues. Plenty of time for side research, this time on Corneille. Did I know Corneille and

Racine were on French paper money? Imagine finding an artist on an American five or ten dollar bill!

"Does Shorty really sit around waiting for Christ to come back?"

"Not entirely. He works for the night is coming, as the old hymn says. The odd part is, he gets this turn-around in a screwy sort of way from precisely the modern far-out theologians he cut his eye teeth on. Have you ever heard of Karl Barth?"

"I doubt it."

"He believed in the Incarnation and all the rest the Bible tells us, without regarding the Bible as infallible. His point was this. Of course the Gospel accounts of the Resurrection are incoherent, but that doesn't necessarily mean they relate a myth. It's a case of sinners bearing witness of a Revelation meant for sinners."

I was guiltily fingering in my pocket some procurer-type business cards I'd had printed up, with "The Merchant of Venus" under my name. It had seemed like a good idea at the time, in fact an inspired gimmick, but I'd changed my mind the moment I laid eyes on the finished product. I'd never worked up the nerve to use them, as I probably wouldn't to show Rose even now. In fact I began to feel thoroughly ashamed of myself as she went on trying to explain an acquaintance who was mystery enough without all the divine ones.

"Barth, you see," she said, I suppose correctly pronouncing it Bart, "argues that the subject of this unique event is God, not man, and only God can know the full truth of his own history. Acceptance by faith is man's only road to this divine history — faith in the reality and truth of what the Evangelists made a mishmash of, with all their beautiful prose. It's a known fact of legal evidence that no two witnesses will agree in their accounts of some dramatic or extraordinarily stunning event, such as an accident or a crime. No one will believe that the discrepancies in the stories proves there was no such event. How much more must we accept on faith the testimonies however garbled to an act of divine intervention!"

"I'd like to walk right on up to our diner. Where we met that night?"

"It's a good fifteen miles."

"Or Feeley's. Where do you go to dinner there? Who takes you?"

"Nobody. I cook at home. I like it. Once in a while we go out; together or with friends. There are some good restaurants in Westport, which is close by."

"Westport! How does Shorty go down, there in Connecticut, I mean with all this meat-and-potatoes Fundamentalism?"

"He goes to Bridgeport. There's a rescue mission there with a foot-pump organ and everything. Where they sing revival hymns and Shorty preaches Christ and him crucified."

We had reached the hotel where she was staying, and we stopped under the yellow marquee. She smiled up into my face.

"Do you go there with him? To the mission with Shorty?"

"Only once in a great while, to humor him."

I shook my head and laughed. "It's like going back to Feeley's, isn't it, after Pierre's and The Palms and all that. Camp."

Now she laughed, looking at the sidewalk, her head inclined. "Shorty's not camp. It's really one of those storefront missions, with a soup kitchen where they give handouts to bums."

"Maybe that's where I'll wind up."

"With your heart of gold." She kisses me on the cheek and is gone, fluttering through the lighted door in her open cape like a night moth.

Going downhill is uphill work all the way, baby cakes. Aaall the way. It was the next day but one that Chuck Everts, this ponce for which Doreen has all the while really been carrying the torch, turns up again, after nearly a year's absence, and I gets the air. Just like that. "I'm sorry, Al. My heart really belongs to Chuck. He's got a lifetime lease on it. It's one of those things a woman can't do anything about. Her heart rules her head."

I'm now so nearly up to my ears in schmaltz I figures I might as well make it complete. I gets stewed, I mean to the follicles, scribbles "Goodbye cruel world," and a few other assorted gems on a piece of stationery, steals down the stairs to the backyard for a length of clothesline, and sneaks back up to my room and shuts the door. I make the rope into a noose, giggling nervously, drag the chair under a chandelier, and tie the other end firmly around the chain hanging from the ceiling. I have my head in the noose when the note I have written strikes me as really not good. In fact bad. A disgrace to the mail order alma mater which instead of fresh lessons is now sending me letters threatening legal action unless I cough up the tuition balance I am reneging on. Hardly pausing to blush with shame, they will send a "field representative" as they call their salesmen, a field representative to pry me out of my grave and the fillings out of my teeth to get what I owe them.

I climbed down and dragged the chair back to the table. That note needed a lot of work. A lot of work. I sat for some time trying to revise it, chewing on the butt of my pencil. It just wouldn't come right. Maybe getting it in shape would keep me indefinitely in the land of the living. My *raison d'être*. That's what it would be. To spend a lifetime trying to get a farewell screed right — what could fill up your allotted span better than that? With my talent I could probably use the combined pump-priming methods of all the artists mentioned in the lesson about getting started, from Shelley's head-heating to Schiller's need to smell rotten apples. Well, I'd certainly taken enough liquor aboard to be in Hart Crane's class.

My pencil began suddenly to fly. "In this world, in which it seems everything is too much and nothing is enough . . ."

I must have scribbled for a quarter of an hour before pulling the chair back under the light fixture again. My pulse was racing. Had been for some time. I climbed back onto the chair. I was fitting the noose around my neck once more when I had the idea that I had been struck from behind by a bolt of lightning. It remained lodged in my chest, a sustained, jagged blaze of sensation. If you can imagine a flash of lightning that stays where it hit, that will give you a rough idea of the pain I felt. I got down and ran to the door. Flinging it open I staggered into the corridor.

"Mrs. Krakauer!" I called. "Oh, Mrs. Krakauer! Hurry, I don't feel well! I don't feel at all well! Get me a doctor, quick . . . There's not a moment to lose."

Hanging wasn't my bag, I realized as I lay in the hospital bed listening to the doctor read back to me the cardiogram which "showed nothing organic." The trouble had been a crisis brought on by extreme emotion. How about an overdose of sleeping tablets? That was a no-no, I gathered from this healer who would give me no more than the one or two needed for a good night's sleep. Well, I would need a few of those to get into the shape necessary to kill myself. That much was clear. You needed robust health for that.

Built up by a few days' stay in the hospital, I bought myself a straight razor which I held to my wrist as I sat on the edge of the bathtub. That went against my grain too. I made a few of the "hesitation slashes" I had read were standard for this ritual. One of the other roomers began banging on the door. "Oh, for Christ's sake, can't you give somebody else a chance?" I called back. "Always thinking of number one. That's you." All this while Mrs. Krakauer was watching me like a hawk. She had of course seen the clothesline in my room and taken it out and burned it. I promised not to "do anything foolish," as well as bought her another line. Feeling sorry for her, I decided the only fair thing to do was move out. I sold the furniture I had put into storage and with the money bought a secondhand car — I had made Rose take our convertible when we split up. I drew the last eighty bucks out of my checking account and headed east.

The trip itself was uneventful except for one narrow squeak at the hands of a speeding motorist on the turnpike. "Want to kill somebody, you crazy sonofabitch!" I shouted as he shot by me at what must have been seventy-five miles an hour. I soon composed myself and settled down to the thoughts that took up most of my waking time.

What in God's name was I going to Connecticut for?

Maybe Rose would know.

9

I had an English teacher in high school who dithered about Bliss Carman, who dithered about the open road. "There is something in October sets the gypsy blood astir." You could as well read February or March being as how the thing is you're on the *go*, and certainly May, which it got to be before I reached Connecticut.

I took my time, picking up hitchhikers and stopping in godforsaken towns to make a few bucks along the way. I had brought along my old brush and stencil set, and with a bucket of phosphorescent paint bought in Indiana I scrounged up a little money printing people's addresses on their curbstones again, as I had in Chi during one of those temporary stopgaps of which my life seemed to be made. Or I'd paste the numbers on rural mailboxes with a supply of decals I laid in. It's amazing how many of us don't have our street numbers anywhere on or around the house. There ought to be a law requiring it rather than the one invoked by countless local constables running me out of town for disfiguring public property without a permit. Once I stopped for an hour in a small-town library to dawdle over a volume of this Bliss Carman. By coincidence he has a passage that shot off the page at me, hitting me in the eye like a jet of grapefruit juice:

> *Heaven is no larger than Connecticut;*
> *No larger than Fairfield County.*

That was exactly the famous county for which I was slowly heading, as slowly as I could, for some reason. A tingle of anticipation, suddenly, there in a corner of New Jersey, made me step on it. I reached my destination the next day. Now we could see whether Connecticut was heaven.

Rowayton, in any case, is a town of seven thousand or so. I had Rose's address and readily found the house she was renting, a standard white Colonial with green shutters. It was dusk of a Saturday night. I slowed passing it, but that was all. I drove straight on back to the main street, which is nothing but a post office and a few stores facing what I first thought was Long Island Sound but is actually the bank of Five Mile River, which

196

empties into the Sound close by. I hung around there watching speedboats and sailboats docking after a day out on the water, fishing crews as well as pleasure craft. I chewed the rag with an old salt in a pea jacket and knitted blue cap, who was on the lookout for an ear to bend. I was only stalling. Now the whole trip out here seemed a mistake; the intended glimpse of Rose's life here, which was its purpose, suspiciously like spying.

I had a few drinks at a bar, inviting the old salt along. He may have followed the sea man and boy nigh onto X-number of years, but all he wanted to talk about was modern educational theories ("theeries" he said, and "idees") which he deemed the "ruination of the young." After buying him two drinks I got back into my car and headed for Rose's place again, still not knowing what I'd do when I got there. I tooled on past and clear to Norwalk, the next town. A guy in a bar there had three or four hats which he was trying to sell. I gathered it was a great hat-factory town. More shades of my past. I tossed down my single drink, drove back to Rowayton, parked the car on the waterfront street, and walked the half-mile to Rose's house.

I slowed as I approached it. Night had fallen, but there was a clear full moon. All the lights in the house were on, upstairs and down, and the road on which I stood watching was bathed in a soft glow. I thought I saw a figure float behind the white curtains far back in the depths of the house, but couldn't be sure. There were no near neighbors. Only one car passed. When it had vanished, I swiftly crossed the road and stole around to the side of the house where it was relatively dark. Further concealed by some shrubbery, I ducked along a short stretch of lawn toward what instinct told me must be a dining-room window. I raised my head cautiously. Standing on tiptoe, I could just peer over the sill and look in.

Rose was sitting alone at a table set for two. She stared without any particular expression at a pair of lighted candles. She blew idly at the flames, making them flutter. She had one hand resting on the table-edge, the other in her lap. She wore a yellow cotton dress I didn't remember. As I watched, she leaned to the right and called something to somebody I couldn't catch, through an open door to the kitchen. From there Shorty materialized, talking and nodding. He had gained so much weight I hardly recognized him at first. He had always been stocky; now he was downright fat. Salvation agreed with him. He wore a dark suit, white shirt and blue tie — apparently the turtlenecks were a thing of the past. He sat down at the other end of the table, folded his hands and bowed his head. So did Rose, more or less as though on cue.

Shorty began to pray. Not the standard perfunctory grace, but a long business in the course of which he raised his head to heaven several times. Among my Chicago boyhood playmates were several Dutch Reformed kids who said their fathers prayed like that at mealtimes. Not just about the food but for everything under the sun — the President, Congress, the poor, the heathen lands and the missions they supported there.

Naturally I was more interested in Rose than in Shorty's string of petitions, of which I could only catch a fragment here and there in any case. She soon raised her bowed head and opened her eyes. She watched Shorty. The way I watched her, she watched Shorty. The whole scene sent a delicate chill up my spine, not alone because of my part in it. I began to feel a little spooked. From her expression you'd think she was about to shake her head. She never did though. Once she reached out a hand to brush something from the tablecloth. Once she scratched her nose. No doubt sensing when Shorty was pounding into the stretch, she lowered her head and closed her eyes again in time for his "Amen." They fluttered their napkins out and fell to.

That was when I had seen enough. This same English teacher had us read *Enoch Arden*. Now I remembered the part where the shipwrecked Enoch returns home after many, many years to find his beloved what's-her-name (Annie?) married to his best friend, Philip I believe it is. Stealing up on their house, as I had just done on Rose's and Shorty's, he looks in on their happiness and — how does that line go again? "Dug his fingers into the wet earth and prayed." That was no doubt what Shorty would have done had the roles been reversed. I went back to Norwalk and got royally stoned. Midway this bender, the question suddenly popped into my mind: Had they had wine with their dinner? I couldn't recall seeing a bottle on the table.

I woke up in my motel with a bad hangover, but a good breakfast of bacon and eggs and plenty of hot coffee did wonders. So fortified, I drove back to Rowayton and wandered down the empty Sunday morning street to the waterfront.

I sat on an upended crate someone had left, staring out across the harbor scene. Seeing the scores of launches, speedboats and sailboats bobbing at anchor in the gray light, I thought: this might be the place. Yes. What pain would there be in a farewell taken only from the element in which it was accomplished? There was nothing here but water, gurgling and gabbling among deserted ships in a mindless dream. There were no people. None of the creatures with none of whom you'd managed to make it. Only their empty toys, for reminders of their absence. Yes, this was It. Let water, the liquid womb from which we came, gather you to herself again. Let water be the curtain you voluntarily draw on the scene . . . forever . . .

"Hey, there! Hi! On for the Audubon?"

I had been mistaken. I wasn't alone. A figure detached itself from the grove of spars, waving. A man in blue dungarees and C.P.O. jacket stood, his legs planted apart in gray sneakers, on the deck of a catamaran. The light caught his thick blond hair and beard, within which flashed a smile whose dazzle I understood only when I had come closer. He was one of those people who clench their teeth when they smile.

So this is Charon, the ferryman who will row me across the Styx, I thought as I scrambled down to the main dock, over the prow of a cabin cruiser and onto the catamaran, grasping his outstretched hand as I sprang aboard. Because the water here was certainly too dirty to take your leave in. It had a grimy, unhealthy look. Somewhere out there it would be cleaner . . . and deeper . . . More hygienic . . .

"What did you say?"

"You're here for the Audubon expedition I suppose."

"Yes. Name's Banghart."

"I'm Captain Spurgeon." He doffed a decayed nautical cap which his golden head had acquired in my few moments' descent. "I don't have a list of the members signed on for the trip, in fact I'm not even a member myself —"

"That's quite all right."

"— I'm just the pilot they hire. But every time I see somebody with a lost look I figure it's one of them trying to find the boat. You're the first. Little early, eh? Well, no, it's already five till nine," he said, looking at his wristwatch. He gazed upward. "Not a good day. Sun'll never get through those clouds, and we may have rain. But what the hell. If those birds can make it here from Florida I guess we can be on hand to watch 'em do it, right?"

"That's right. Whcre do you reckon we'll go today, Captain?"

A few questions and I had myself briefed. Spurgeon piloted members of the local chapter of the Audubon Society out among the innumerable islands dotting the Sound for a spot of bird watching. Up to now they had rented all manner of craft, but today I gathered we were trying out a catamaran the chapter was thinking of buying. A catamaran is a raft on two hulls. This one, named *Preserver III*, was a platform of about ten by twenty feet, on what you might think of as two outboard motorboats. I don't know where *Preservers I* and *II* are, but I can make a pretty good guess. Two short backless benches running parallel in the middle were all the seating space available for the ultimately eighteen passengers — or "souls" as they are called in the case of ships that go down. Enoch Arden is good!

I don't think there's any such term as "waterlubber," but it'll do for the majority on deck who fancied themselves a cut above landlubbers. When Mr. and Mrs. Liederkranz, between them in the neighborhood of six hundred pounds of solid Teutonic flesh, sprang aboard, we nearly sank right there in the harbor. I dunked a shoe in the drink when himself lit on the fore starboard corner where I stood, staring out to sea as a means of keeping my back turned to the chapter members now streaming down from shore, one of whom might have a reservations list to check the passengers against. None of them did though. The craft was balanced again once the Liederkranzes were symmetrically distributed for weight. Next came the chapter president, a hearty scoutmaster-type from the breast pocket of whose tweed jacket the bowl of a pipe protruded, like the head of a baby kangaroo from its mother's pouch, who bulldozed us all into calling him Bim. I never did find out his name. Others now swarmed aboard who will be named as occasion arises, but of course dangling from nearly every neck was a pair of binoculars, reminding me of the cop who had nabbed me for short-arm inspection in the park. They all packed lunches too, making me wonder how long I would be stuck on this packet. It was hardly ten minutes past the hour set for departure, nine o'clock, when Spurgeon cast off lines in fine nautical style and, the twin outboards churning in our stern, we went sliding along the gray river water out to the Sound.

"Laughing gull at two o'clock," said Captain Spurgeon, pointing.

"Aye, aye, sir," I said, wanting desperately to belong.

The rain he had promised began, a faint, nagging drizzle that gave him the first thing not to be daunted by. Others came in rapid succession once we got out of the relative safety of the harbor and out to open sea — or what might as well have been open what with most of the islands that normally dotted it becoming shrouded in mist. The rain stopped, as often as you've quit smoking, for the first time now, but the islands disappeared from this cozy little offshore deal. I worked my way around to where Captain Spurgeon stood very erectly at the controls.

"Which one did you say we were headed for again — sir?" I asked.

"I thought we might make Cockenoe, but I think we'd better put in at Chimon."

"Let's do that then," I said, though both names had an

ominous ring to them, frankly. Like the sort of places where deep calleth unto deep at the noise of His waterspouts, and all His waves and billows have gone over us. That type of thing.

What we were going to do on Chimon, we were going to see if there were any rats left there. It seems we had gone out there as a group on prior occasions to pour poison down every hole and run we could find, in hopes of eradicating the rodents and thereby protecting terns nesting and breeding there. I gathered the rats preyed on the eggs and also the young.

The mist was now so thick and the visibility so short that navigating for any specific island was a little like calling a pool shot without being able to see the pockets. But Captain Spurgeon knew these waters like the back of his hand, and after a bit there was Ulalume, I mean Chimon, looming up ahead of us only a shade off course, which he corrected with a fidget of some relevent dohickey. The trouble came trying to start the starboard engine up when we were ready to leave, about an hour later. We had seen no rats in that time, but no terns either — though whether because it was too early for them to be nesting or they were all out on a little gad of their own I didn't ask. I followed the others around the island, listening. "Of course *gulls* will eat terns' eggs too," Bim said.

"Of course," I said.

He lowered his binoculars to get a closer look at me. "I haven't seen you around before, have I?"

"No, I'm from Chicago. I belong to the Chicago chapter. I heard about the splendid things you folks are doing here, and thought I'd come see for myself. I think you folks are doing a bang-up job. Tell me, do you have much trouble with egrets around here, Bim?"

"What do you mean 'trouble' with egrets? What trouble could they possibly be? We love egrets." He peered suspiciously at me.

I thought it was a safe question because it was plagiarized from one I had overheard a woman asking a moment before, a Mrs. Bonga, from Norwalk. I imagined now that I had misunderstood — she had undoubtedly meant the trouble they had getting egrets to *nest* here. I should have known, of course, from the trouble we'd gone to to get the rats *out*. I mumbled a revision of my own query along those lines, but it wasn't necessary. Spurgeon was calling Bim from the shore just behind us, and he turned and excused himself. I edged around to where they stood in consultation. Spurgeon was frowning and held a rag in his hand, with which he had apparently been trying to dry the engine.

"You say you're sure the manufacturer raised these goddamned engines after that trial run?" he said.

"I'm positive," said Bim. "He raised them three inches."

"He should have raised them six or eight at least. I'd have seen to it if I'd been running her. They're still much too close to the water. And the sealing on these hulls doesn't look the greatest to me either. The top of

205

this one is beginning to come away from the underside of the deck. I understand this is a new model they're experimenting with?"

"Those are the first hulls run off the new molds. They're guaranteed to last a lifetime."

"Oh, they probably will!" answered the captain, with an odd laugh.

I didn't like the looks of all this. When he finally got both engines going and we all tumbled aboard and shoved off again with the pole, I sidled and jostled my way into a position directly beside the captain. The wheel at which he stood, erect and doughty like the hero in a saga of the sea, was a few feet forward and between the engines in the stern. It was connected to a panel, or dash, where the shifts and throttles were. After over-hearing him mutter what I thought was enough about "overcorrecting" this and that till he "got the hang of her," I posed my question.

"You mean this is the first time you've driven this pile of kindling?"

He nodded looking not at me but down over his shoulder at the crippled eggbeater — for it had conked out again. Another thing I wasn't too crazy about was the sight of Bim, down on all fours, peering into the hold of the starboard hull, accessible through a hinged trap about two feet square. In the depths of this hatch I could make out one life preserver. This little old washboard wasn't very well named, was she then, if that was all those orange weskits she carried? Bim leaned away down to look as far as he could into the prow of that hull — which as I say can be visualized as one of two rowboats on which the raft set — so that his own aft stuck up into a fine rounded target to plant your foot on, in default of being able to kick yourself there for signing on this maiden — and probably swan — voyage for the local Audubon Society. Because he backed out of the hatch and said:

"Shipping water over the top of the hull."

He closed the trapdoor, marched across the deck to the other, shouldering his way through assorted Bongas and Liederkranzes, pulled it open, kneeled down and peered into that hold. I tried to see past his shoulder to make a weskit count in there, with no luck. "This one's O.K.," he said, climbing to his feet. "So far."

"Oh, ginger peachy," I says.

The scoutmaster air was gone. He gives me a glare of the kind Ben Bolt must have made Sweet Alice tremble with fear at. "I don't believe I got your name," he said.

"Al Banghart."

"I didn't realize you were a member."

"Of the Chicago chapter — remember? We do this all the time on Lake Michigan. We out there keep hearing of the bang-up job you're doing out here, Bim." Too bad I couldn't have sent him a record of this testimonial, as a keepsake for his heirs and assigns.

Only half of the "souls" on board heard this exchange, or followed Bim's examination of our floating cellars; the rest were intent on Captain Spurgeon's hind-end as he bent over the stern yanking the starter cord on the broken Mixmaster. Again it caught, and for another interval we chugged along through waters grown suddenly choppy. The rain resumed, harder than ever. By now of course all thought of island hopping was over — getting across to the mainland in as straight a line as possible became the order of the day. People opened their lunch hampers, mostly for the hot coffee, though a few gnawed disconsolately on sandwiches and drumsticks. Suddenly there was a faint snapping, or ripping, sound from the port hull, the one just given a clean bill of health by Uncle Bim. It reminded me of descriptions given by passengers of ships striking icebergs. "Like a can opener cutting into her side." Bim was on his knees at the open hatch. He was joined by two or three others. The sight struck you as so similar to a prayer meeting that I smiled at the shivering Mrs. Bonga and said: "Crap game."

"Same trouble," Bim said, getting up. "Just not a good sealing job between the pontoon and the deck. We're certainly learning a lot on this trip! They talk about still getting the bugs out of her. I guess the Audubon Society isn't going to buy this catamaran."

"I guess not," I thought.

The water was now pouring into the front of the first hull faster than it could go out the weephole in the stern. Or whatever they call them. Scuppers I guess. And it wasn't long before the steady slap of the choppy surface had the second hull in the same fix as the first. We began to wallow. We rocked from side to side as well as pitched from fore to aft and back again. Waves sloshed over the deck, which sank lower and lower from the weight of the water accumulating in the bilges. Two women leaned over the edge to be sick. All this while, people continued to peer out through binoculars that couldn't possibly have meant anything in that mist. Force of habit I suppose.

Bim sprang onto one of the benches and called for our attention.

"First, I want to say this," he began. "It goes without saying that the minute we get ashore we're going to launch an investigation."

"I always figure dry land is the place to launch anything if you have to," I pipes up. I was trying to keep everyone's spirits up, and a sense of guilt down in my own case. I supposed it was unfair of me to be taking up my weight on a raft threatened with sinking when I intended to kill myself anyway. It was just that, once out on the water, I had swiftly added it to my list of media unacceptable for an exit. No, *sir*, my whole being said, thanks just the same. Yet if worse came to the worst, it seemed I must eventually sacrifice myself.

A woman with a pocket transistor radio had tuned in a local revivalist. "Brothers and sisters, have you found Christ? Oh, come to Him before it's too late . . ." *Shorty?!* I strained to catch it, but glares from her shipmates made the woman turn it off before I could check my suspicions.

"Now, I know what you're thinking," Bim resumed, "but let's get one thing straight. Those hulls can't possibly fill up fast enough or high enough to cause us any real trouble. There are two blocks of foam — Styrofoam, you know, like some of your picnic hampers there — two in each hull, which together give us three thousand pounds of flotation. I repeat, three thousand pounds of flotation. Oh, they may send her back to the factory and raise that a little, but that's how much weight we can carry now. This cat can't sink. *She's unsinkable.*"

"Like the *Titanic*," somebody muttered.

"Goddam it, will you shut up!" snapped a Fred Laycock, Jr., of Darien. "You live your life doing the right thing, never step out of line, oh, maybe pad the entertainment on your income tax a little or renew a magazine on a special offer intended for new subscribers only, but basically honest and decent, always playing fair and giving the other fellow a chance, and this is how you wind up."

A rangy man named Cartwright had taken out an envelope and a pencil and was doing some figuring. He did it with such purpose everyone watched him. How he kept the envelope dry enough in that pelting rain to write on was a mystery. He was soaked to the skin like the rest of us, but the gray hair hanging in his eyes gave him a special look, like an English sheep dog performing a feat of intelligence. I kept looking around for signs of other craft, a passing power launch, a fishing boat, in vain. I thought of the poem about how man's control stops at the shore . . . something something sinks down with bubbling groan . . . what was it? Unknelled, uncoffined, and unknown. Oh, we would be knelled, coffined, and known, all right, but a fat lot of good it would do us.

Cartwright had reached the end of his computations. He cleared his throat authoritatively.

"If, say, our average weight is a hundred and seventy-five," he began, and we all tried not to look accusingly at the Liederkranzes who between them accounted for a quarter of our total tonnage and probably brought that mean figure up from something more like a hundred and fifty where it belonged, "then the combined weight of all eighteen of these bodies is thirty-one hundred and fifty pounds. Or a hundred and fifty more than her official capacity, quite aside from the dinghy there, which must weigh another hundred, and our picnic gear and other equipment."

He turned questioningly to Bim as chairman of the chapter and by extension responsible for this junket. But Bim was not to be stared down. He had a question of his own.

"Eighteen? Why eighteen? Where do we get eighteen? I don't have the reservations list but Newman told me the tally was only sixteen. With Captain Spurgeon it would come to seventeen. Who's the" — he gave a kind of hideous effigy of a good-natured grin as he gazed around — "the stowaway?"

I clapped my hands together and shot an arm up into the air.

"I know what we'll do!" I said. "We'll tell each other stories. To pass the time, till help arrives or we limp into port or whatever. You know — like in *The Canter-bury Tales?* I'll begin. All right, let's try to relax, every-body! Sit down on the benches, those who were, and the rest at ease while Captain Spurgeon wipes those spark plugs clean, or whatever he's doing."

They all quieted down, and I began, to a congregation swaying slowly in unison, their color ranging from gray to green.

"Once upon a time there was a mysterious lodger in a rooming-house in a large city. He was silent, speaking to no one, remaining by himself much of the time. He would speak only when spoken to, and not always then. Newcomers to the house, and anyone meeting him for the first time, always asked about him. They were told that he had a secret sorrow. He had once played the vio-lin, but now no more, not since a certain tragedy befell him — whatever it was. His heart was broken. That was the story. Since the day of his heartbreak he had not played a single note. He would never play again. The instrument in its plush-lined case lay in a corner, gathering dust. He would never open it again."

Several of my audience were looking past me toward the stern, more interested in what was going on there. Bim and Captain Spurgeon were poring over a nautical chart, murmuring about the relative depths of the wa-ter among the islands and channels and harbor points marked on it. They had it spread out on the "reserva-tions lectern" as I thought of the dashboard panel, be-cause it was the same height and shape as the slanted desks where stood the despotic maître d's with their guest books in my restaurant period. My life seemed to be passing before my eyes even before I had hit the briny deep. I continued my story.

"One day a young man came to room in the boarding-house who was determined to get to the bottom of this Bird Who Would Never Sing Again. Seeing him stand at the window gazing sadly into the streets, or pensively sucking on his pipe in a corner, or, as it happened often, going for long walks in the rain, he resolved to make work of it. 'I'll find out what broke his heart if it's the last thing I do,' he said.

"Well, it was hard getting a lead on him, a place to begin. But one day he met someone who remembered the name of the conservatory at which the heartbroken artist had studied, and he went there by bus. From a girl in the office with access to the files, he learned the name of the violinist's teacher — a Professor Fahrenheit. Though old by now, Fahrenheit still took on a few special pupils. Those with some talent. He opened up when he learned I — when he learned the caller was a friend of this Duane Decker, as I'll call him. He took him for coffee in the school cafeteria. 'Ah, ja, Duane. Old Duane. How is he now? Not too goot? Dot's too pad. Zolitary spirit, ja? Still? Crushed by zome zorrow you zay? Must get zome conzolation from de old fiddle though. What, never puts bow to string? I can't understand dot. He was mad for dot fiddle, it was his whole life. At least he wanted to make it his whole life.'

"Fahrenheit was thoughtful as he packed his pipe. He shook his head. 'Dot was what I had to give him ze what-do-you-call-it about. Ze moment of truth.' 'What do you mean?' the other asked. Fahrenheit got his pipe going and leaned back in his chair. 'After five years study here, two mit me, he got me aside one day and said, "You know, Professor, I have concert stage ambitions. It's all or nothing with me. You've heard me long enough. Lay it on the line. Have I got what it takes?" Dot was when I had to tell him. To enchoy life, lend it some shine, to delight his friends of an evenink, maybe play mit a nice logal orchestra, he's plenty good enough for dot. But ze concert stage, no. Dot final somesink, call it spark, cheenius, vat you will, he ain't got it. I had to lay it on ze line.'

"Fahrenheit puffed some more, looking at the caller through the smoke. His pale blue eyes widened. 'Lieber Gott, dot's de zorrow he ain't played a zingle note zince? Himmel! . . . Ach me . . .'

"The young man went home with a heavy heart of his own. Now he, too, had a sad secret. One he, too, will carry to his grave."

Which will be a pretty watery one, I thought as I finished. They all sat or stood in silence on the foundering raft. Bim and the pilot were still consulting the chart and looking through binoculars for islands they couldn't see with the naked eye — or with the glasses either for that matter. As we watched, the single motor still going pooped out. Bim shouted through cupped hands, "Ahoy there!" A returning shout was so vague it could have been an echo of his own. Someone began singing *Nearer, My God, to Thee.*

"Who's turn is it now?" someone else said. "Something more cheerful. You, Bob, tell us a story. Tell us a funny story."

Bob Wilson was the type of which I imagine there is one in every such party. It's his wife who's a nature lover, he just goes along. A card, at some point he'll say, "Ornithology is for the birds," or, "Look, everybody, a double-breasted seersucker!" He's got a million of 'em.

"There was this guy, this veep who's used to everything being specialized. So he calls this commercial bakery one day and asks to speak to one of the vice-presidents there. 'Which one?' says the switchboard girl, and he says, 'The one in charge of cookies.' She says, 'What kind of cookies?' He says, 'Fig Newtons.' And she says, 'Which kind, California or Smyrna?' "

Mrs. Laycock brust into tears. "It's what Fred says. He's right. What have we done to deserve this? You do your best, the right thing, and you wind up like this. All because somebody's on board who shouldn't be."

"Now, now, that's not the whole trouble," Wilson said. "There are lots of factors. Not the least of which is that this Tinker Toy is coming apart." He readjusted his stance on the wallowing craft.

"But he may be the margin of safety. He may be the last straw."

"She's right," Laycock said, laying a hand on his wife's shoulder. "And I think we should find out who he is."

"I believe Mr. Schmulka has a story," I says, fairly. "Let's give him a chance. Let's try to give him our undivided attention, shall we? Do you have a story, Mr. Schmulka?"

"I certainly do."

He was a wiry, intense little man whose slant on everything was political. He belonged to the Audubon Society the way he belonged to the A.D.A. His interest in ecology was mainly a war on the forces plundering the planet for private gain. He hated the vested interests more than he loved birds, though he probably loved birds.

"My story is the story of a country," he began, giving a fidget to a drenched cap the peak of which he had bent into a saucer shape that carried the surplus rain out over his eyes, like a spillway. "A brotherhood, called the United States of America. It was born in 1776, out of the fires of revolution. Gradually that was lost sight of, as the opportunists, the exploiters and the fat cats took over, and changed her from the brotherhood she was to what she is now. Millions in poverty or discriminated against or both, the land despoiled, the waters polluted, the air unbreathable, the consumer swindled. Petroleum slicks on beaches whose once beautiful sands are strewn with the carcasses of oil-deceased birds. The comely mountain valleys of Kentucky laid waste by strip miners permitted by law to rape the earth for monetary gain, and destroy the farms of decent and hard-working people into the bargain. This is what has become of our brotherhood."

There was no doubt the raft had become a soapbox,

but, sitting tailor-wise on its edge, Schmulka had every-one's attention. He shifted on his sopping bottom and continued.

"Well, we are about to celebrate not only a birthday but a centennial — our second. We are a few years from our two hundredth birthday, and how close to our origins? Are we still a nation dedicated to the ideal that all men are brothers? No! for alas the patriots are tuning up. The my-country-right-or-wrongers, the mindless occupants of cars reading 'America, Love It or Leave It.' Fools and blind, blind to what we have become. A nation of plunderers at home and abroad, committed in Asia to a government that is a military autocracy. Yes, here we are," he said, raising his arms, "two hundred years after our own Revolution, marching shoulder-to-shoulder and side-by-side with King George III!"

"Oh, now, just a minute, brother."

"Don't you call me brother."

We polarized out there. In the political free-for-all the story hour erupted into I drifted (good word for it) over to where Spurgeon and Bim were again in conference. The harbor chart, in a stiff transparent sheath, was propped against the dashboard pedestal. I made nothing out of a perusal of it till I overheard Captain Spurgeon identify a small gray hump materializing on our starboard bow as Cedar Hammock, which my eye just happened to catch on the chart. He had very skilfully managed to maneuver us among rocks and reefs in relatively deep water, but here it was only three and four feet deep, and in some places only a foot or two. Also we were a mere five hundred yards or so from shore. This seemed as good a spot as any to make my supreme sacrifice.

Tilting both engine propellers up out of the water, Spurgeon now began to pole toward shore. The depth tabulations on the chart were correct, as far as you could see using the pole he was plying as a measuring stick. After a few minutes Bim relieved him. They both looked pretty grim. The *Hesperus* pitched and heaved worse than ever, though you trusted the water got progressively shallower as we wallowed along toward shore. Then the pole-as-rule wasn't measuring a foot or two of water at all, but nearly its entire length. Bim had to squat to use it. Had he been getting his purchase on rocks before, and now on the true bottom? Had I read the chart wrong? Another thought flashed into my mind.

"Captain, are the chart measurements based on low tide or high? Or some average? Or what?"

"Mean low tide," he answered without turning.

"How much can high tide add?" I asked with a gulp, as though I had already swallowed some of this element through which we miserably inched.

"Six to eight feet."

"I see. Then at high tide, where it says one or two feet you have to read nine or ten."

"That's right."

I was about to ask the sixty-four-thousand-dollar question — what stage of the tide this might be to the best of his knowledge — when somebody else remarked, "This is all over my head."

"Or will be soon," I said, and dubbed in a laugh for everyone's benefit.

"*Will* you shut *up*," repeated this Fred Laycock (the guy who had always tried to live right, padding his expense accounts only slightly and never tearing off of mattresses those little tags the removal of which is forbidden by law, and this was his reward). Spurgeon opened his mouth to say something, but whatever it was he intended to keep the conversational ball rolling with we never learned. Nor had I the chance to call over with an encouraging smile to the handful of women now bundled into what had been dug up in the way of life preservers, "All dressed up and no place to go are we?" Just then there was a slosh of water over the deck not to be entirely accounted for by a marked increase in chop, though there was that.

The exact sequence of events here is confused in my mind, but of course that wave must have followed the sharp ripping sound suddenly audible under our starboard, which gripped the entire passenger list with the suspicion voiced by whichever of our number shouted, "The right hull is breaking completely away! Oh my God!" That touched off a general stampede to larboard, where the sudden load dunked us momentarily up to our ankles. That was the wave. My own panic was fired with boyhood memories of my grandfather's tales about the excursion steamer *Eastland*, which tipped over in a Chicago harbor because of an overload on one side.

Spurgeon had to seize quick and firm hold of what was now the next thing to a mob on the brink of pandemonium.

With amazing cool, he took stock of the crisis by evaluating factors in it that must have been fed into his brain with the speed of light. The rush to larboard hadn't been all that unlucky. It served to correct the drop on the starboard that resulted, or would have resulted, when the pontoon on that side collapsed, losing us our buoyancy there. There was of course some flotation provided by the deck itself, but too little to count in an emergency like this. A deckside minus its pontoon will go down. So will a deckside with all the passengers concentrated there on a shipshape craft. But all the passengers huddled on the *good* side can help correct the list on a crippled. At least so it seemed here. After the first sloshing dip on our larboard had righted, through some counter-bulge in the stew beneath us, maybe something in the rhythm of the chop itself, the weight concentration there created a fluke in our favor that Spurgeon instantly tried to capitalize on. Instead of redistributing his pack of shivering wretches, he ordered us all as far over onto larboard as we could go, and in an even line, the heaviest sitting on the very edge of the deck with their legs hanging in the water. The good hull there, being set a few feet in from the edge, served as a kind of fulcrum, helping tip the other, disabled, side up just barely out of the water into which it would otherwise have sunk. Think of a badly designed teeter-totter. Among those ordered to sit on the outer rim with their feet in the water were of course the Liederkranzes, the male half of whom was jabbering things like, *"Wir gehen der Ewigkeit entgegen!"* — roughly, we're heading for eternity. Well, we would see.

With our balance thus precariously restored, Spurgeon took the pole from Bim and resumed shoving us toward shore. "All right," he said quietly as he heaved steadily, rhythmically away, "now let's all keep our places and hold still." My own speculations raced on through my head. Wouldn't it be just as well to lose the other hull too, if and when we reached wading depths? It might only ground us in waters a raft as such could be pushed through, say by the men with the women on board. Did the footage taper uninterruptedly all the way in to shore? Or might a "soul" slogging it through shoals at chest or knee level suddenly drop into a pothole and be no more? I visualized a dozen John the Baptist heads on one rather dirty pewter platter, then only the platter. A hymn came from the woman's transistor: "Sweet hour of prayer, sweet hour of prayer, that calls me from a world of care . . ." Bim bit his lip, watching Spurgeon pole.

"Probably a responsibility you've never had before, and never dreamed you'd have, eh, Captain?" he said. "Getting eighteen people safely home from a shipwreck."

"Only seventeen now!" I cried out, and leaped overboard. "God bless you one and allbrgub . . . lub . . . urb . . . urble . . . glrb . . . b . . . b . . ."

10

I came to between clean white sheets, under a ceiling of lime gelatin. A black nurse was bending over me whose morning-glory mouth I might later as a matter of interest care to explore, like a honeybee in quest of nectar, then having plundered that flower . . .

"Well. There you are. How do you feel?"

"Weak. Otherwise O.K. Where am I?"

"Norwalk Hospital. You had a close call, fella."

"Why, what happened?" I asked, figuring I should brief myself on the official version.

"Besides nearly drowning, you hit your head on a

rock. You're just lucky the water wasn't very deep there, so they had no trouble fishing you out."

"Oh, wasn't the water very deep there? I just don't know very much about these harbors . . ."

A question nagged me with lunatic irrelevance: why did the boat already have a name? The Society hadn't yet bought it, who would have been its first owners. Boatbuilders surely never christened craft themselves?

"Or maybe it was the edge of the boat you banged it on. Nobody seems to know. In all that confusion . . . Here, see?" She took my hand and guided it gingerly up to my brow, which I felt to be swathed in a medical turban. "But forget it now for a while, hear? Thing is to get a little nourishment into you. How about it, think you can eat something? It's supper time."

"Do you know a good place we can go?"

A bar or two of laughter from the trumpet mouth. "I see yawl quite yourself again."

"For what it's worth."

"I see. The modest hee-ro. Wait till you read about yourself in the morning paper. Head'll probably swell right out that bandage. We shooed all the reporters away. Figured they could get all the dope they needed from the people in charge of the party. You'd be the last one to give any sensible account of what happened, seeing you been out from the time they fished you out of the water till just now."

"Tell me just one thing, nurse. Is everybody else all right?"

"All fine. Soaked to the bone, but I think that's about all. Shook up some, of course, but outside of that . . . Look, the resident's going to have a look at you, then you have some supper and a good night's rest."

"You're not going to show me the sights?"

"You're plenty enough a sight yourself. But you'll be O.K. in the morning. We'll keep visitors away."

"Do that by all means."

I slept well, under some kind of sedation, had a lumberjack's breakfast, and read the story on the third page of the Bridgeport morning newspaper.

A tale of heroism and nearly fatal self-sacrifice climaxed a boating disaster yesterday in which a party of seventeen bird watchers and their pilot nearly lost their lives in usually humdrum Rowayton harbor. The group were members of the Audubon Society exploring nearby islands on the maiden voyage of a newly constructed, and recently redesigned, catamaran, already christened *Preserver III* by the boatbuilder in full anticipation of its purchase by the local chapter of the Society. "I guess we're not going to buy that cat after all!" said a spokesman for the chapter who preferred to remain anonymous.

What happened was that her twin hulls came loose as a result of improper sealing against the raft-like deck, owing to the use of a calking compound being test-marketed, like that particular model of the craft herself. Water filled the hulls faster than it could run out the scuppers in their sterns, where the two outboard motors conked out in the general seawash. An overload of passengers was another factor contributing to the ultimate foundering of the vessel. It was this discovery that prompted one of the passengers, Albert Banghart, 29, a visiting Society member from Chicago, to sacrifice himself by jumping overboard. Reports of his last words as he hurled himself into the icy waters varied. Some said he shouted, "Only seventeen now!", others that he cried, "This is on me!" Still others swore that he exclaimed, "Hope you make it, friends. Nice to have met you all. God bless you!"

Make it they did, even after stopping to fish out Banghart, who had struck his head on a rock and been rendered unconscious. A passing motor launch heard the shouts of panic through the thickening mist and put about, finally towing the crippled vessel into the Cove Marina. Fortunately for Banghart, the waters were relatively shallow at the point where by chance he elected to jump overboard.

The manufacturers, who are located in north Bridgeport, could not be reached for comment.

Passengers, gratefully drying themselves in their homes and in nearby taverns, recalled how Banghart had also tried to keep everyone's spirits up and calm their fears when trouble developed. He got people to take turns telling stories, in the manner of the pilgrims in Chaucer's *Canterbury Tales*, and also cheered them up with his quips. When an argument over Vietnam was punctuated by a cry of, "There's a grebe!" Banghart ironically chaffed, "I'm glad there's something around here besides doves and hawks."

I put the paper aside and stared up at the lime Jello ceiling. That in the corridor resembled cottage cheese. How did plasterers get that charming nubby effect? . . . My mind drifted, itself rudderless, back to my old problem, that of getting myself into shape to kill myself. You had to be in fair trim for that it seemed. In fact topnotch form. The phone rang, evidence that at least they considered me well enough to take calls. That was some progress.

"I see you're in town."

"Rose. Where are you?"

"School, of course. Nice going. Are they treating you right? In the manner you justly deserve?"

"Royally. I must make more contributions to hospitals. The nurses leave nothing to be desired."

"Or at least you'll see to it before you're through with them. Look, what brought you here?"

"My car."

"I see. Inscrutable."

"I thought you always found me scrutable enough."

"Well, I'm damn glad you're here, Al. I really am. So when can I come to see you?"

"I don't know what visiting hours are."

"I'm sure they'll let a wife in any time. Anyway my last class is at two o'clock. See you then?"

"Please omit flowers."

During the three hours or so till she came, I pondered the problem I was now really faced with: whether to take back a woman who, having discarded a no-account, returns to collect her hero. It seemed to boil down to that. Were women after all everything their detractors said they were? Grasping at bottom, thoroughly selfish, acquisitive, using men to serve their own vanity, out for the main chance? Oh, what a mare's-nest it all was. What a hoax. What a tissue of illusion a sexual relationship was, what a web of pretenses and deceits and little prettifications. Why should I take her back? Why not send her packing? Why not, really? I gave a little wriggle of pleasure: at least for once I was negotiating from strength.

She arrived a little after three, carrying a basket of fruit wrapped in cellophane. Cunningly packaged herself in a gray tweed suit with a red muffler flung around her neck. It was a bright day, but windy, I could tell that from the trees thrashing at my window.

"Hello, Al. How are you?"

"Ready to leave. Thanks for the fruit. It looks good. Don't mind if I do." I tore off the crackling cellophane and ate a banana. "Been a good year at the college?" I said, peeling it down.

"Swell. They're renewing my contract. With a slight raise." We sparred like this for a while, and then she broke down. "What brought you out here, for God's sake?"

"I thought I needed a sabbatical. You know — from the strains of being a bum."

She laughed at that and pulled her chair up closer to the bed. "You can imagine what a surprise all this was to me." I could sense her reining in her emotions as she turned ironic and said, "I didn't know you were a bird lover."

"I plan to watch the quail going by the corner drugstore again, soon as I get out of here."

The nonsense talk went like that for five or ten minutes. I finally satisfied her curiosity about how I got into

227

the expedition. "Just mistaken identity. The pilot thought that's what I was there for. Actually I was just a water-front character loafing around."

"You planned to call me, I presume?" she said, looking into her hands. "Or were you just . . . ?"

I figured the cues should come from me, and the clues from her. Setting the banana peel into an ashtray, I said, "What about us? How do you feel about things, after a year out here?"

"It all depends."

"What do you mean?"

She rose and walked to the window. She stood there for some time, twisting the blind-cord in her fingers and looking out. Then she spoke.

"Are you a creep?"

I reached over to the basket for an orange and started clawing the rind from that. It was a little hard to answer a question coming that suddenly and that deep out of left field, even just to ask for clarification. She volunteered that after several moments of the silence broken only by the sound of my dismantling the orange and then popping segments of it into my mouth.

"That time you were arrested. I believed your sporting-house raid story then, but now I've begun to wonder. Whether there mightn't have been something else. Something in the park. The officer didn't specify, except to hint that there was an incident. You don't have to tell me in detail what it was — little girls or what-ever — just to level with me. I think you owe it to me to tell me the truth." She turned around from the window. "I thought about it very little at the time, but since then it's come to haunt me. Well? Are you a goof?"

This was absolutely fascinating. I wouldn't have missed this for the world. I began gesturing well before I had anything to say, not that I wasn't curious myself till the very last instant what I would hear. I swallowed the section of orange I was chewing and said, "Let me answer that by asking another question. Would it make any difference?"

"Well, yes," she answered, slowly, but not because there was any doubt in her own mind about what she wanted to get off her chest. "A woman might leave a philanderer, or a goldbricker, or one of those husbands who just can't be housebroken. Even one who drops in for a visit to The House of the Rising Sun. She might get just plain fed up with someone who just can't keep his hands to himself, or pass up anything in skirts, or however you want to put it. But no woman deserving the name would walk out on a man who's sick."

I lowered the orange in its paper napkin onto my stomach and stared at a spot on the wall. The blood in my circulatory system stopped. It came to a complete standstill. It paused, then slowly reversed itself, flowing in the opposite direction. Is this how the hero at last collects the heroine? A little more of this Alice in Wonderland logic apparently dominating a woman's heart was in order so that he might first collect his own senses.

"What about Shorty?"

"He's hopeless. There's nothing anybody can do for him. He's beyond reason, out of reach. Of course he's feeling no pain. God-intoxicated. 'Tipsy from salvation's bottle,' as Dylan Thomas puts it." She sighed. "I mean he's slipped off into another realm, or dimension, where I just can't connect with him. Nobody can — except his own kind. He'll probably marry one of his converts in the end and they'll live happily ever after. That lets me out, of course. It's obvious you need me more — as I probably do you. Anyway, I'll never cop out on anybody. That at least will never be said of me."

I shook my head, at the same time patting the bed, on which she sat down. I extended the orange on the paper napkin to her. She helped herself to a juicy segment while I did the same with another. We munched silently away together, gazing rather blankly at one another, in the peaceful sunshine and shadow of the hospital room.

11

That was how we resolved it. I flew back to Chi long enough to wind everything up there for good and all, for of course I had to move east to where Rose's work keeps her, for these years at least. I have a new kind of work of my own, that I'm hopeful about. This is how it developed.

We bought a house there, one of the white Colonials typical of Connecticut, and trying to call a plumber to fix a broken drain one day, I got an answering service. Nothing unusual for repairmen there. Then I phoned another plumber at his home, and was asked by a woman, "Who's calling please?" Brother, I thought.

But not too amazed. I once telephoned a farmer there and got the same thing — "May I ask who's calling please?" This was a dairy farmer on whose property mine what-do-you-call-it — abuts? I wanted to ask which of us might be responsible for the repair of a fence running between us, through which some of his cattle were straying onto my piddling two acres. A third try for a plumber finally got me onto him via a short-wave phone he had in his mobile shop. A carpenter I needed shortly thereafter was even harder to reach, and curter when I did. He agreed to pencil me in for the first of the month. An electrician was absolutely unlocatable. Some again female voice, whether domestic or at an answering service, said he was in Bermuda and was not expected back till the middle of the following week. It was then that the inspiration hit me: what these boys needed was an agent.

So that occupational elite, skilled labor, have now got one, at least in my corner of Connecticut. They almost all have unlisted numbers — plumbers, electricians, everybody. All calls are funnelled through my office, there to be sorted out by me as to priority, urgency, credit rating, and so on. It's a great responsibility, and a growing one, for me and those following in my footsteps — for the idea is spreading to other privileged communities. I have got to know not only my stable of clients, but their customers in turn. I am getting quite familiar with most of the housewives in town, their problems, their temperaments, the degree of their tendency to exaggerate the need being reported and the service requested. I must be able to evaluate, say, a hysterical call saying something has gone wrong and the first guests are beginning to arrive, and so forth and so on. I myself *am* a guest, very often, circulating among other guests careful to cultivate and maintain my favor, as a man wielding all this power. Almost any day picked at random will offer a representative glimpse of my life, and of this side of our present-day culture.

I will get to my office at nine. I may water a potted plant sent around by one or another of the local ladies trying to keep in my good graces. On the morning in question an amaryllis adorns my desk, its huge bloom spread wide from inner ovules, the stamens with their pollen-sticky anthers standing big and stiff within the gaping pink orifice. Rated M for mature audiences. The phone rings and it's Mrs. Montgomery, up to her recently lifted chin in water in the kitchen to hear her tell it. It's only a drain she can unclog herself with a dollop of a commercial preparation I can name, but it's against the ethics of my profession. Besides she may spill some of the sulfuric acid of which it mainly consists on those lily-white hands, requiring a doctor nobody on God's *earth* can put her in the way of. "I'll try my best to reach Mr. Haley," I say. That's the one out in his mobile shop (of which there are now two branches tooling about the countryside). Next Mrs. Cooney, unable to get her washing machine started. Well, tough taffy, try plugging in the cord, that sometimes works wonders for our dumb bunnies. Meanwhile I'll try to reach one of our experts in the field. Last time she called was New Year's Day because the furnace was out. Dead. Kaput, the house cold as a witch's tit, and her poor mother ill with flu under a pile of blankets and overcoats deep enough to bury the old thing alive in. That call was made to my house direct. Because Home Services Unlimited, the name of my agency, has an emergency number in the book. When I finally got an oil furnace man out there, justifiably hungover himself, it turned out that the furnace switch was off. That was all. A drunken guest at party revels the night before, groping along the wall for a light switch on his way down to some swappable wife waiting in the game room, had flipped it off. We stuck her for the forty-five-dollar triple-time-for-holidays fee.

One day you get a really legitimate plea and you get on your horse, as I did following an S.O.S. from a housewife I quite like, Pam Talbot. I drove out to the artisan needed to fix a broken step her aged father had already nearly broken a hip on. This was the carpenter Jack O'Keefe. He is a slick-haired black Irishman of thirty-some, handsome, an awful snob. I found him eating his lunch on the second-story girder of an addition to a choice piece of shore property he was working on at the time, his back against a stud. He conducted his half of the conversation looking down at me from up there.

"Mrs. Talbot has to have some work done as soon as possible," I said, squinting up into the sun.

He closed his lunchbox and lit a cigarette. "She has such terrible skin," he said, snicking the match away.

"What the hell has that got to do with it? Be a little

234

reasonable, how about it. You can knock it off tonight in an hour, and you'll get your double time. You're very fond of that. Christ, that's twenty bucks an hour. How about a little infinite understanding?" I buttered him up with an Agnew story, him being a reactionary into the bargain. "These punks with their Indian love, they aren't a patch on Spiro for sincerity. He *means* it. He's an honorary member of a tribe. You know which one, of course. The diatribe."

"Her father will bend my ear about the old days in Secaucus. New England, how it used to be. Who needs that?"

"I'll see that he's out of the way. I'll personally guarantee it. Talbot can drive him around for an hour or so."

"You mean if he makes it off the bar car straight up?"

"Bill's on the wagon these days. And you know what a dish she is otherwise."

"So do you, you bastard. Well, all right. But I won't give an exact time, and no flat fee."

"Done and done. You're an angel."

It can be seen from just this brief snatch of one day how important my work is — how valuable that type of service, in this day and age. So I try to keep familiarized with all concerned. I make frequent visits myself to the homes from which these housewives are calling, to evaluate for myself the urgency of the needs reported, the validity of the requests, to be fair and intelligent in determining the priorities there must inevitably be, on a backlog of work always as long as your arm. Many's the cup of coffee I drink in the kitchen, though nothing beyond that, so far. Well, there was one little episode that did develop, one narrow squeak culminating in a moral rebirth of the kind I hope I'll never sink so low as to be incapable of, I mean should the occasion arise. Which I hardly think it will!

Mrs. Plowditch is a patron of the arts who awoke one morning to find her kitchen more teeming with cockroaches than a Dali painting. Now, pest controllers favor a kind of liquid spray that seems to do the job just a shade short of the absolute extermination that would rule out repeat calls. At least such is the impression I got in my bailiwick. But I have one man who uses a fog that will purge your house a hundred percent — leaving him free to pursue his commercial jobs, such as the beer and soft-drink trucks he's retained to treat twice a week (*la cucaracha* likes that glue in the six-pack cartons). This is where the question of integrity comes in. A literary agent may represent any writer he thinks will make money, ditto a theatrical agent any ham he can keep working. I won't do that. I will only take on craftsmen of proven probity and skill — besides maintaining a personal interest in the client at the other end. When Mrs. Plowditch called to be put in touch with a good man, the urgency in her voice had me galloping over to see what I could do myself.

Tess Plowditch is a female of very high voltage, as well as one of the kindest women I know. She insisted on being gagged when we made love, so her outcries, quite uncontrollable in her peaks, would not reach the ears of her poor dear invalid mother-in-law confined in a nearby bedroom. There was another complication. Mrs. Plowditch's fingernails are of a length a Chinese mandarin would be proud of. And what delicious caresses they can bestow! Except that in the course of these self-same raptures, when she doesn't know what she's doing, she may claw your back to ribbons, leaving long red welts difficult to explain at home. Unless you happen to be Mr. Plowditch, as I am not, nor aspire to be. I have my own jewel, thank you. Anyhow, I soon saw that gagging Mrs. Plowditch would not be enough. You would also have to tie her hands behind her back. It was the only safeguard, she admitted it herself. In fact she insisted on it. Even so, another hour's refuge from the greed and perfidy of the world.

So we were making love in this way, one afternoon, when I sensed her uttering noises through the knotted handkerchief in her mouth that differed radically from the muffled outcries I was accustomed to. Also, she seemed to be rolling her eyes and jerking her head upward toward the door. I finally realized she was trying to tell me something.

I got to my feet, in time to hear the motor of a car shut off outside. I ran to a spare bedroom across the hall, from a window of which I could look down in front. To my horror I saw two men sitting in the front seat of an automobile talking. The one behind the wheel was gesturing around, as though explaining something about the house and grounds to the other, who nodded and smiled. The husband unexpectedly bringing a friend home for dinner was the cliché that struck me like a thunderbolt. Plowditch would not have been able to reach his wife to tell her because she always took the phone off the hook so as not to be disturbed!

I flew back into the other room, passing Mrs. Plowditch on her way to make the same check, and got into my clothes with a speed that would have done credit to a fireman. "Is your husband dah, dah, dark with thick bla, bla," I bleated in a strangled squeal not unlike Mrs. Plowditch's through the gag. She stood in the doorway, naked and insane, her mouth still stuffed, though working hideously behind the muzzle. When I started to untie her she shook her head violently from side to side, mumbling more frantically than ever. Evidently her mind was working at a speed more lightning than mine. Because she had a plan. In the fragment of time I had the handkerchief off she whispered, "No, leave them! I've been tied by a —" "Burglar," I finished, digging what she meant and knotting the handkerchief again. It was while fastening the last of my clothes that I doped out the escape plan that constituted my half of the solution.

Leaving her bound and gagged in a chair, I snatched up a portable TV set and one or two other small items and shot on tiptoe down a flight of back stairs long ago earmarked for just such a contingency, out the kitchen door and around to the garage. It was behind this that my car was parked, out of view of the one standing in the driveway before the door of the house. So far so good. I sneaked into the open garage, shifting the loot under my arm, and up to a window through which I could again see Plowditch and his friend. They climbed out of the car as I watched, Plowditch still on his house-tour spiel, the other nodding along. Now this was the dangerous moment. The next few seconds would decide my fate. If they strolled around back here, I was a gone gander. Yet it was for such a development all our prepa-rations had been made: my discovery, or at least the "glimpse caught of me as I escaped." The stolen goods in my hands as I fled, together with Mrs. Plowditch's trussed-up condition, would authenticate her story of a robbery. That was the idea.

I stood frozen in my shoes. Yet though physically paralyzed, I was still mentally able to run through all my options at computer speed and evolve an alternate plan to shift to in any upset at this juncture. If the "in-truder was surprised," he would drop the boodle, run to his car and peel out of that driveway at a speed that would leave them goggling open-mouthed until he was gone. Luckily it was a circular drive with two exits, and I might just have enough of a start to foil pursuit and capture. That would remain to be seen. But a sudden bolt proved unnecessary. They went on into the house, exchanging some remarks about the high price of top-soil. I gave it a good fifteen seconds, enough for them to be well inside with the door closed behind them. Then I drove out slowly and with as little noise as possible, flooring the accelerator the instant I jerked out onto the road and headed for the tall timber. It was only after

239

five or six twisting turns and backtracks, with my eye on
the rearview mirror, that I was sure nobody was giving
chase. I stopped at the Plenty of Fluids for a couple of
stiff ones, sinking into an empty booth with a sigh of
relief and a prayer of thanks to God — and a vow that
I had now, finally, beyond the shadow of a doubt,
learned my lesson. My tomcat days were over. This was
It, mucking-about-wise.

I had soon regained my composure enough to evaluate the day's shambles and salvage a small prize for my
self-respect. One thing could be extracted from the sordid tangle of events leading to this moment that was to
my credit. Stealing the stuff I had. Because why had I
agreed to simulate a burglary in this fashion? For myself? No. For a woman's honor, and the peace of mind
of another. It was mainly Rose I wanted to spare the
discovery of that intrigue, and at all costs — at the price
of a terrible personal risk. Because such a revelation
would have meant nothing to me except maybe a couple
of black eyes from an irate husband, whereas being
caught as a housebreaker would have meant who knew
how many years in prison. Think about it. I had chanced
all that for the woman I loved. You could even say that
snatching up that television set was my finest hour. Or
I should say moment, for it was a split-second impulse
I acted on, and therefore doubly commendable, since
we are normally not at our best when obeying split-
second impulses, they being usually matters of self-
preservation such as fear or anger, or self-serving like
lust and greed. I had many such to be ashamed of in

my past. This was one in which I could take pride. And it was in that light, as a sort of test of character I had passed, that I saw it as settling some of those old and humiliating accounts. Yes, the most decent thing I have ever done is steal a television set. And that's it. Chivalry is not dead. There is hope for the human race.

These were my thoughts, alone there at the Plenty of Fluids, in this crucial afternoon of my life.

But why was I always running? So many recollections of flight and escape came back to me now, all wound around one of my grandmother's words, "skedaddle." In panic I had skedaddled from my fiancée, to whom I was now skedaddling home in the form of a husband. In terror I had skedaddled out of Mrs. Landgrabber's kitchen only to face her defoliated husband in my own. Could I have fended Plowditch off with the same act I had used on Landgrabber? "Mmyes?" Hardly, under the circs. That was one of Beverly Wainwright's ghastly abbreviations, that had in the end sent me skedaddling in her case. Just a sec, don't be ridic — now it was Women's Lib. Tena Tate was much too intense, I knew I'd had it with rapture, it was the warning signal, when I heard her exclaim over her letters one day, "I *love* mail!" Skedaddle. In finally breaking off with Faith Mullins, after the muddle about the Burton-Donne record, I ran down her front porch steps amid valedictory protests that she'd never have let me go that far if she hadn't understood I was Catholic. "Didn't you tell me you were Catholic?" "In my tastes." Skedaddle. Memories, memories. How they came flooding back. I vowed this would be my last skedaddle, to or from calamity, this really terrified flight in the dead of winter. It had snowed, so beautifully, then frozen, and now the earth was the same sugar-coated ball of mud it had been in Chicago. Gray clouds, through which the sun dimly burned, like a frosted electric bulb. I had to watch my driving, the roads being glazed with patches of ice so much more treacherous than a solid sheet.

I realized where my instincts were taking me. Toward the edge of town there was a Salvation Army collection bin in a vacant lot, a good place to dispose of the swag. I was donating some mighty fine articles, I reflected as I opened the flap and dropped them through the slot. Besides the portable TV there was an electric clock and an attractive crystal paperweight. I couldn't help shaking my head as I added them to the mountain of broken toasters and castoff garments with which people fancied they were being charitable. Then I went home, a chastened man, turning over a new leaf he had every confidence would be his last.

Of course I couldn't go *directly* home, exactly. I had to check in first with my secretary, whom I have to leave in charge of the office when I'm out, among other things. I always hold my head down between my legs for a few moments before calling her into my inner office, so that when she gets there the blood will have flowed into my face, giving it the healthy flush that makes a man more attractive, at least than he is with his normal winter pallor. This afternoon I had some letters to dictate (including one about a possible branch office in a nearby city for which I had a partner spotted). I got firmly rehearsed in my mind what I wanted to say, sat doubled over with my head between my knees for a minute or so, reached up to press the call buzzer on my desk, waited a few seconds more as I heard her footsteps approaching, and straightened up just as she entered my office. "Shirley, would you take a couple of letters please?" Miniskirts were all the rage then, and I could look at a pair of beautiful drumsticks as I dictated. Oh, she's more than a pretty face.

That I have shaped up doesn't mean I don't have wayward notions. No man is without those, certainly. I must say some of those Connecticut women into whose homes my work takes me, not to mention Shirley herself of course, stir up many a lingering afterthought, inspire many a woolgathering hour as I lie in bed at night waiting to fall asleep. I believe the French have a term for it, *derrière-pensée* or something like that. I must ask Rose about it.

So the years slip away, like water down a winding stream. Rose is delighted I'm busy, and very, very profitably so. Though I sometimes seem to sense she thinks I deserve better than to be a ten percenter. Or maybe that she deserves better than a husband who is one. But why? Bram Stoker was an actors' agent (he handled Henry Irving among others) who went on to write *Dracula*. So you never know. Who can tell what will develop? Anyway, she herself has great continuing prospects as an educator. With high hopes for me. She has every confidence I can win through and realize myself, as you know by now. Because the potential is still there. That nothing can ever change.

One thing I don't understand to date. It's one too many for me. What she means by saying chivalry isn't dead thanks to women. I always thought that was supposed to be a man's virtue.